NEWBIA

Chelee Cromwell

NEWBIA

Tellwell Talent

www.tellwell.ca

ISBN

978-0-2288-2285-1 (Paperback)

Table of Contents

The Beginning

The sun was soon to set over the mountains. It was 5:45 p.m. I was cleaning the front counter when I heard my name being called.

"Nyria."

A soft voice spoke, coming from behind me. Karen was hovering over the dirty dishes that were left behind from my previous customers.

"These need to be put into the dishwasher, Nyria."

Karen was the type of boss who never seemed to have many emotions when it came to most of the other employees. But she took very kindly to me for some reason. I think it's because I reminded her of her own daughter, Emily.

Emily was killed in a car accident two years ago, and ever since her accident, Karen has seen me as a replacement. Maybe because I was the same age as Emily, and we loved the same things. Nonetheless, Karen was definitely one of a kind.

I turned to her while yawning.

"I'll bring the dishes back when I'm done cleaning the counter."

As I finished cleaning, I darted to a table where I found four plates with what seemed to be numbers written on each of them in BBQ sauce.

They read "2014."

"That's weird."

As I continued cleaning the table, someone outside the diner honked their horn. It was my best friend, Scott Merritt. Scott always picked me up after work, but today he was a little early.

I saw his awkward, long hand reach outside the car window to wave at me. I smiled then gave a quick wave back. Scott was a very young-looking thirty-year-old with jet black hair and big green eyes, unlike me—a short, average-looking twenty-four-year-old with short dark brown hair and brown eyes.

Scott and I had been friends for about three years now and he takes me as his little sister. He is the only child in his family. He always wanted someone to protect, and I'm it.

After putting the dishes in the dishwasher, Karen held her hand out to me in a fist. It was full of my tips for the evening.

"Here sweetie, here's your tips."

As I reached out for them, I whispered quietly, "Do you think it's OK for me to leave early?"

She gave me a nod yes. I smiled and swiftly grabbed my jacket while I headed for the door.

As always, the corner of the front door bumped the diner's sign. It now hangs down, from all the wind we've been getting lately.

As I plopped down into Scott's 2002 Sebring, he began to giggle.

"When is the owner ever going to fix that damn sign? Didn't it used to read Dartmouth Diner? Now it reads Dartmouth iner. Who would eat in a Dartmouth iner?"

Laughing, I gave him a hard punch to the shoulder and told him to drive.

"Why did you pick me up so early?"

"We're picking up Lisa from the Sportsplex and going to the new pet store in Bedford. I want to get her a kitten today and I'm sure you want to be there too. You guys can do your ooh's and ah's over them."

"Oh that's right, you forgot her birthday last week. I guess it's make-up time, eh?"

I was being little sarcastic. He looked at me as if to say shut up, so I did. We were waiting patiently for Lisa to get off the bus. We noticed a settled look on her face, then a smile as she noticed me in the car.

"What are you doing here, Nyria?" she asked as she climbed in the back seat.

I looked at Scott waiting for him to reply so I didn't give the surprise away. Scott hurried to answer.

"We're taking you somewhere and leave it at that."

She motioned the zipper movement over her mouth.

The car ride was quiet, no one saying anything. We were all excited about our journey. Pulling up to the pet store, Lisa yelled out, "*Oh my god!*"

Both Scott and I looked back at her to see what she was yelling about.

"I know why you brought me here. I'm getting another kitten, aren't I?"

Scott was the first to answer.

"Well, we know you love cats, Lisa. So I thought we'd come here to get you one."

"Yeah, since he forgot your birthday," I mumbled under my breath.

Lisa jumped out the car and ran to the pet store. As I got out of the car, Scott grabbed my arm and asked me if I was still having nightmares.

I didn't answer him right away.

"Yes. We'll talk about it another time, OK?"

The nightmares had been a constant nuisance since my birthday two months ago. The night of my twenty-fourth birthday was one of the worst nightmares I have never had. Nothing bloody or gruesome—I always seem to be chasing something or someone. Or was I the one being chased?

The nightmare was always taking place in the same spot: in a cloud of trees. Fog covered them like a blanket and there was movement, but it was never mine. I would wake up in sweats from it and very disoriented.

As Scott and I opened the pet store doors, Lisa already had an all-white kitten in her arms. It had one blue eye and one brown eye.

"That's an ugly kitten," Scott announced.

She ignored him, shoving the kitten into my chest.

"Isn't he a little cutie, Nyria?"

I didn't have time to answer. The kitten looked straight into my eyes, as if he knew me or sensed something about me. He jumped out of my arms onto the floor, curling up under the closest shelf.

"What the hell was that all about?" Scott yelled with a puzzled look on his face.

I shrugged my shoulders as Lisa went to recover him. The pet keeper came over quickly, asking if everything was all right. Lisa assured him things were fine and that the kitten jumped out of my arms because he was scared of all the excitement.

Quickly, I moved toward the cash register, as if to tell Scott *Let's pay for this kitten and get out of here before something else happens.*

As we were leaving, I felt something following me. I looked back—Scott and Lisa were the only ones behind me. No one else was leaving the store or entering.

I gathered my thoughts and asked Lisa if she was happy with her new kitty. She smiled and thanked us both. I smiled and told her you're welcome. Even though Scott paid for it.

Scott dropped Lisa off first, where we gave our normal kisses and said our goodbyes. With just Scott and me in the car, he reached over and patted me on the back.

"So what about those nightmares?"

I smiled a bit, and with a sigh I replied.

"Yes, I'm still having the nightmares. They don't make sense, though. I'm always in the same place and it feels like someone or something is there. When I look around it's only trees with fog all around them."

He nodded, stating, "You know, people's mind can play weird tricks on them."

My eyes moved back and forth watching his expression. Then I cracked a smile.

"You're probably right."

He didn't say anything more, he just looked at me from the corner of his eyes, making sure there wasn't more I wanted to say.

We drove up to my building's back steps where he usually drops me off. I leaned over and said goodnight and gave him a kiss on the cheek. He reached over to stop me, saying, "Call me if you need me, OK? *OK?*"

I put one leg out the door while saying, "I will. Love you. Goodnight!"

Shutting the door, I headed for my apartment.

I undressed, got into my PJs and slumped on the bed with exhaustion. My eyes started to close, and the next thing I knew I was back in the same nightmare as before.

Bit something was different. Someone was standing at a distance.

The fog still covered the trees like a blanket, but this time I didn't feel like I was searching for something or someone. I felt complete, as if this person was a part of me. I couldn't see his or her face, only their outline.

By the way it was standing, I guessed it was a man. He stood with his hands down by his side and feet planted on the ground. His silhouette was muscular and tall, maybe six feet.

My curiosity was overwhelming, so I started walking toward him. As I got closer, the trees seemed like they were hugging me and the fog got thicker.

Just as everything seemed to be closing in on me, he reached out for my hand, still standing at a distance. I hesitated for a second but felt comfort. I started to bring my right arm up and something struck me in the chest like a punch.

My lungs! I was grasping for air. The trees had their branches around my chest and the fog was covering my face. I couldn't breathe.

I felt a warm body against mine from behind, saying. "Breathe, Nyria, I'm here now. Nothing will hurt you when you're in my arms."

As I struggled to take a breath, my lungs opened. I shifted my weight to one side so I could turn around to see whose arms I was in.

Just as my eyes started to focus on the figure holding me, I woke up, and took a gulp air.

"Shit. I didn't get to see him."

I wanted to know more. I tried to go back to sleep.

When I finally got back to the dream, the nightmare was gone. But I wanted to see him again.

"Why was he gone, what happened?"

As much as the nightmare bothered me. I wanted it to come back so I could see him, even for a second. I felt warm and safe when he was there and now . . . nothing.

Beep, beep, beep!

My alarm clock screamed.

I was overtired but I managed to get to my feet. I turned the shower on, and thought about him again.

Who was he? Where did he come from? What did he want? Why was my nightmare gone now?

These were questions running through my head as I washed up to get ready for my morning shift.

Heading for my apartment door, I glanced in the mirror.

"Ugh!"

My eyes had black rings under them.

"I'm sure Karen will have lots to say about my rings."

I locked my apartment door and looked down at the pink rubber watch my mother had given me for my twenty-fourth birthday.

"Crap, it's 6:28. I'm going to miss the bus."

I ran down the hallway and out the front doors as the bus came over the top of the hill.

Running down to the stone-hut bus stop, I dropped my apron without noticing.

Out of breath, I leaned on the pole that held the bus sign in place. The doors opened and a deep voice called out, "Late again this morning, I see."

"Good morning to you as well, Jack."

Jack smiled and waited for me to take a seat. I sat in the far back of the bus with my head against the window. The ride wasn't long, maybe twenty minutes. Jack always dropped me off a few feet away from the diner. As I made my exit, I thanked him once again. He gave a wave as I stepped off the bus.

I entered the diner and Karen was there to greet me.

"Good morning, sunshi—"

She didn't finish her sentence as she looked at my eyes.

"Long night, Nyria?"

Hanging my head down, I managed to say, "Yeah . . . a very long night."

As I continued walking, eyes were following me as if everyone was seeing a ghost. Bev piped up, saying, "Look at what the cat dragged in—ha!"

Being arrogant as usual, I see. I didn't pay any attention to her, as always. She got under my skin, but I had to work with her. So ignoring her was the best thing ... for her.

I walked to the back of the diner and put my things in my locker. Rummaging through my bag, I noticed my apron was missing.

"Oh! Bloody hell! I must have dropped it when I was running."

A hand reached around me from behind.

"Wear this one, but I want it back at the end of your shift."

Karen winked at me and laid the unused apron on my shoulder. "Thanks."

It was a beautiful Friday morning and the diner was busy as usual. Businessmen coming in for their morning coffee and construction men swallowing down their food without chewing. I was always on guard when they were around. I was scared that one day one of them would choke from not chewing their food properly.

The afternoon was busy on that day. A construction company was building a strip mall next to our rundown diner. I was cleaning tables as fast as my hands would let me, and placing orders as customers arrived, making sure no one waited more than ten minutes for their orders.

Smiling and greeting customers was one of my talents.

Anyone who sat at my designated tables was pleased by the customer service they received while eating here. I was making good tips. Bev always seemed to compete with me, but she lost every time. He who laughs first laughs last, I thought to myself as she rolled her eyes at the sight of me. I'd always smile back, but deep down I hated the sight of her face. My mother always told me, "Kill people with kindness." So that's exactly what I did.

There was now an hour left of my shift. By this time the exhaustion was creeping up on me. Customers were paying for their food, exiting the diner satisfied. I was cleaning the coffee maker when I noticed something from the corner of my eye.

I tried to focus on the statue in the distance, staring out the big picture window that covered most of the front of the diner. A tall muscular figure stepped out from the shadows behind the trees and started walking toward the diner, almost as if he was gliding.

I couldn't take my eyes off him. He was so beautiful. Dirty blond hair, baby blue eyes and a squared-off jawbone.

I was studying him so hard, I didn't even notice he had opened the doors. He was now standing on the inside of the diner with a gorgeous smile from ear to ear.

I thought for a second. *No, it couldn't be him. It was just a dream.*

I was conversing with the little voice inside my head.

I was just about to greet him when Bev blew by me like a bat out of hell, blocking my view of this beautiful creature.

"Please take a seat. My name is Bev and I'll be your waitress. Would you like a drink before you order?"

He didn't answer her. He took a step around her with something in his hand.

He was now standing in front of me holding what looked like an apron.

I was stiff as a brick wall, like I'd seen an angel or something. My stomach had butterflies and my hands were sweaty, probably because I was squeezing them so tightly, trying not to stare at him.

But he was so perfect.

"Excuse me, I think you dropped this this morning," he sang out like a soothing hymn.

I didn't move; I felt lifeless. Catching myself, I cleared my throat.

"Thank you."

I did not take into perspective that I had dropped my apron early that morning. Bev butted between us, still trying to get his attention. He looked at her then stated very nicely, "I'd like for her to be my waitress. Thank you."

With a *whatever, I don't care* attitude, Bev turned toward me, nudging my shoulder as she pushed her way past, talking under her breath.

I smiled at him as he smiled at me, still showing his straight white teeth.

Mesmerized at his beauty, I gathered my thoughts and gestured for him to take a seat in the middle both. He didn't take his eyes off me as he sat down.

"Can I get you a drink, sir?"

"Please. A coffee with one cream. My name is Sebastian Brinks."

He was holding his hand out waiting for me to take it, and reply back with my own name. I wiped my hand on my borrowed apron, then reached my hand out to meet his.

"Nyria Crowell."

Before he let my hand go, he pulled me toward him without much effort, whispering. "I need to talk to you."

The Stranger

He held my hand with a genuine look in his eyes as I replied. "Me? You, you . . . need to talk to me? About what?"

He didn't answer right away. He glanced around the diner to make sure my ears would be the only ones catching his words.

"After your shift, can we talk? This isn't the time nor the place."

Letting my sweaty hand loose, he smiled, showing his pearly whites again.

I contemplated for a second then began to stutter. "Y-yeah. Yeah, sure."

I moved slowly toward the coffee maker I had just cleaned. I grabbed a mug from beside it and poured his drink.

I glanced back at him once or twice, to find him marvelling over me. It felt nice to have such a gorgeous man wanting to talk to me, as I had only seen myself as an average girl.

Before I took the coffee to him, I noticed Bev at his table trying to make conversation. He did not look up at her as she talked. His eyes followed me wherever I went. He seemed fascinated by me.

Bev noticed he wasn't giving her a second glance. She turned around, swinging her long blond hair as she strutted past me.

Laying his coffee in front of him, I asked if he wanted to order.

"We are closing in forty-five minutes, so if you want something to eat I need to take your order before—"

"No. Thank you, this is great."

Still smiling, I walked to the counter and started cleaning up again. I did not want anything holding me back at the end of my shift.

"It's all done, Karen. I'll see you Monday," I yelled to the back of the diner.

She was on the phone but she gave me a wave and blew me a kiss to say have a good weekend.

Grabbing my coat, I headed for the front door. I didn't even remember to grab my tips on the way out.

I looked to where Sebastian sat, but he was gone. He must have paid for his drink to wait outside for me. I turned the corner of the diner, stalling until I got where he was standing.

He was leaning against a 1996 beige BMW.

"Wow, this is nice. My kind of car."

Smiling, he stood proud. "I knew you'd like it. I can drive you home if you want."

I wasn't paying attention to what he said exactly . . . *I knew you'd like it.*

I would never get into a car with a stranger. Even a good-looking one. But the words came out quicker than I thought possible.

"Sure. I just have to call my friend so he doesn't come to pick me up."

Not taking my eyes off him, I stared as he glowed in the sunset. I called Scott, got his answering machine. I left him a message not to come get me.

As I shut my cell phone, Sebastian walked toward me. Opening the passenger-side door, he seemed to be captivated with me. His eyes following my every move. I leaned down to see the inside of the BMW. It had wood grain throughout.

With no hesitation, I sat firmly in the sports car, and he closed the door behind me. The seatbelt was automatic, and it moved to lock itself into place.

Opening the driver-side door, he climbed in.

"So, what did you want to talk about?"

I was more curious than I've have ever been.

"Before I tell you what I need to say, you have to promise me something."

He paused for a second, studying me, waiting for my answer.

"OK, what?"

Turning the ignition on, he put the car in reverse. I waited patiently for him to start driving. I knew he was trying to concentrate on backing up, so his response wasn't going to come at the exact moment.

When he finally approached the main road, he glanced at me before saying, "This is all going to sound bizarre and outlandish but . . . I need your full attention, without any interruptions until I'm done, please."

"Yeah, sure."

I started to feel a little bit skeptical. But it was too late now. I was already in his car.

Unaware of my optimism, he took a deep breath and began.

"OK, well, you already know my name. Where do I start? Um, OK, I'm . . . I'm not from here. I—"

"Where are you from?"

He gave me a look of disappointment before saying, "I thought you said you wouldn't interrupt me."

I had to apologize, because that is what I promised.

"Sorry. Go ahead."

"OK. My name is Sebastian Brinks and I'm not from this place. I come from a different realm called Newbia. Newbia is an outside realm that created Earth for our seeds to grow. Seeds being you . . . humans."

I stared at him as if I were caught in a dream. He wasn't paying attention to my face, and he continued.

"My kind cannot have children unless they're made on Earth first, by the men of Newbia and women like yourself. After the children are born, they are brought to our realm where they become like me, a Newbian. I am of human descent of course, though we are more aware of the gifts we have. We live in a different realm, as I already stated. And there is no hate toward our fellow beings, absolutely no chaos. Unless, of course, we do a crime while on Earth finding our seeds. Meaning, if we do something bad, any misdemeanour while we are here, we will pay for the consequence when we return back home to Newbia."

He glanced over at me and found me speechless.

"I told you it would sound a little bizarre, but please listen, there is so much more."

I thought I was on Candid Camera. I continued to humour him, while I laid my cheek in the palm of my hand.

"We—meaning you and I—were conceived and born at the same time. I was born here on Earth just as you were, but I went to Newbia shortly afterwards with my parents. I grew up there knowing you, feeling all the emotions you were feeling. Dealing with everything you went through as you lived your life on Earth. I know almost everything about you. But you seemed to block me out when you turned eighteen. This has never happened before, to any Newbian. Which left me feeling empty for six years. You're so different."

I was waiting for him to stop and say *Gotcha!* but his expression was serious. I turned more toward him, listening to him speak.

"I will die here on Earth if I am not with you, so . . ."

I had to interrupt him. He was starting to scare me when he said the word *die.*

"Um, this sounds very interesting, but you can let me out now."

I felt my intuition climax to its peak.

"Please don't be scared of me. I would never hurt you in any way, for you are mine."

I screamed, "*Let me out now!*"

He pulled to the side of the road and took my hand while I was trying to open the door.

"Nyria, please just listen to me."

I pulled away from him, struggling to get the door to open.

"I don't know who you think you are or what you want from me, but stay away from me."

I rushed out of the car, slamming the door behind me, and ran toward a crowd of people walking. I tried to stay in the midst of the crowd so this crazy but gorgeous man wouldn't do anything to me.

He rolled down his window and drove alongside me, talking in a low whisper.

"Please Nyria, I will die here if I'm not with you. I can only be away from you for no more than four days. I need you to listen to what I have to tell you. I will never harm you, I swear."

He couldn't continue anymore. I was far enough away from the car that he had to do what I asked of him, which was just one of the rules Newbians had to obey. They have to do whatever their seed tells them to do, unless it means doing the wrong thing.

I didn't know any of the rules yet, but I soon would.

He noticed I wasn't coming back to the car but he continued to plead for me to listen. He finally drove away with disappointment written all over his face.

He was now out of sight. I took a deep breath of relief and headed for the nearest bus stop just in time to catch my local.

As I reached my apartment building, I glanced around to make sure he didn't follow me home. He was nowhere in sight. I scrabbled through my bag to find my keys. Sighing as I found them, I hurried in.

Opening my apartment door, I threw my bag behind me and ran for the phone to call Lisa.

"Lisa! Can you . . ."

That's all got off my lips when I heard a voice in my head. *Nyria, please don't tell anyone about me. I will never hurt you.* Then the voice was gone.

"Nyria! Nyria!" Lisa screamed at me through the phone.

"Nyria, you there?"

I didn't answer her right away. I was wondering how I heard him in my thoughts.

"*Nyria!*"

"Oh, sorry Lisa, I'm here."

"What's going on? You OK?"

I waited to reply back. I didn't really know how to explain what just happened. Plus, having him in my head was disturbing and out of the ordinary. The only thing I could come up with right away was, "Yes, I'm fine, I . . . just wanted to see if you were OK. When I was on the bus I seen an ambulance at your building and I wanted to make sure it wasn't you."

That was a lie. There was no ambulance. I had to come up with something quick so she didn't think something was wrong with me.

"It wasn't me, Nyria. I didn't see any ambulance either."

"OK, just thought I would check. I'll talk to you later," I quickly responded, then hung up the phone. I heard her say something before I hung up, but the dial tone was already sounding.

She called me right back, very confused.

"Nyria, you sure you're OK? You just hung up on me."

"I'm fine Lisa, I just had a long day. Can I call you later?"

"Sure, go get some sleep, girl, you seriously need it."

"OK, will do. Talk to you later."

I could hear him in my head again.

I need to talk to you, please! I can't be away from you four longer than four days.

I blocked him out of my head, realizing suddenly I could do that. I paced back and forth in my living room, not knowing what to do next. I went to the balcony doors and cracked my curtains open. I saw him standing alongside a tree with his hands at his sides.

This looked a lot like my dream. Was he the one I was dreaming about?

Fog began to roll over the adjacent building, covering the trees like a blanket.

"Oh my god, what is happening?"

I opened my balcony doors and peeked my head out, exaggerating with my lips so he could read them.

"Go away, or I will call the cops."

He was now back in my head again.

I told you this would sound bizarre, but I need you to believe me. Calling the cops is only going to make you sound like you're losing it. I won't be able to get you out of the mental hospital if you do.

I didn't want to hear him anymore. I shut my balcony door and closed the curtains. I needed to block him like I did before, but he was trying his hardest to stay in.

"Please, Nyria."

"*No!*" I screamed out loud, but he didn't stop.

I will stay away from you at a distance. I cannot promise you I will go away forever.

That was the last thing I heard him say.

Can he hear me if I talk in my head? Or can I only hear him? I pondered this as I continued blocking him as hard as I could. Finally, nothing but silence.

I plopped down on my sofa. I was curious and scared at the same time.

"What do I do? If I tell someone they will think I'm crazy for sure. He even said it," I thought out loud while massaging my temples.

I decided to go to the fridge to grab a drink. I was so thirsty. I stood up against the stove and continued thinking to myself.

"All he wants me to do is listen. Maybe we can . . . no, I can't!"

I was fighting with myself now. My eyes were getting heavy. I knew my visit to the sandman was soon to follow.

Slouching my way into my room, I grabbed my PJs and threw them on. I glanced out my bedroom window to see if he was still standing there.

I couldn't see him anymore. That didn't mean he wasn't out there. He did say he wouldn't stay away forever.

I had to get some sleep. Maybe he would get the picture and be gone by tomorrow morning.

I lay on the sofa, tossing and turning. I couldn't sleep, not with the thought of him stalking me.

Slowly, I got up and crept to the balcony doors.

Why was I so curious?

I opened the curtains to see if he was still out there. Sure enough, there he stood, gazing up at my balcony doors. Almost as if he knew I would appear.

I stepped out onto the balcony and leaned my stomach against the railing. He started moving forward slowly, slow enough that I wouldn't get scared and rush back in.

"If I hear you out, will you leave me alone?"

He shook his head and replied, "If you hear what I have to say and you still want nothing to do with me, I will leave. But, I should let you know . . . I will have to stay on Earth and die. I cannot go back to Newbia without you."

I didn't want him to come into my house. Nor did I want to go outside where he could do something, anything to me.

Where could I talk to him where I felt a little bit more comfortable?

I gave him an option.

"Meet me at the mall tomorrow or at the park down the street. You pick."

With no hesitation, he answered, "The park."

"OK, I will meet you there at nine a.m. Now, will you leave me in peace?"

He smiled, and I heard his voice in my head again.

Yes. Sleep well and I will see you tomorrow.

Stepping back, I grabbed the curtains so I could duck under them to walk back into my apartment.

I glanced back to where he was standing. He was gone. Where did he go so fast? I thought.

Doesn't matter, he's gone now. Maybe I can get some sleep. I plopped down onto my sofa. I lay there for a few seconds, then was out like a light. My sleep was very peaceful. Not a nightmare in sight.

What Does He Want?

Waking up to the sun shining through my blinds, I looked at the clock hanging above my balcony doors. It was 8:51a.m. "Shit! He's probably waiting for me."

I jumped up off the sofa, dashed into the shower and washed up quickly. I wanted to get this over with.

As I dried off, I opened my top drawer, throwing on the first thing I found. I didn't noticed that I was not matching until I reached the building doors to go outside, looking down at the brown jogging pants and the purple tank top I was wearing.

I shrugged my shoulders as if I didn't care. Taking in a deep breath, I began to walk down the street toward the deserted park.

I thought there would have been kids playing, but I didn't take into consideration that it was Saturday and kids were probably sleeping in, something we all did when we were younger. The weekends were sleep-in days and play until Mom decided to call you in.

There he was. Sitting on the park bench with his arms folded across his chest. As soon as he saw me, he smiled and stood up.

I slowly walked around the fenced park toward him, keeping a distance.

"OK, I'm late but I'm here. You have fifteen minutes."

He coughed and cleared his throat.

"Why do you think I'm here to hurt you? I could have done anything to you already if I wanted to. But I don't wish to hurt you in any way."

I stayed planted where I was, just in case this was some type of trick.

"Go on, I'm listening."

Before he began, he stared at me with a smile on his face, but his eyes were glaring at me, as if he wanted to approach me.

"I don't want to take other means to make you listen to me. I want it to be your own free will."

What did he just say to me? My own free will? Huh?

I interrupted him before he could say another word.

"What do you mean my own free will?"

He cleared his throat again and said, "There are things I can do as a Newbian. One of them is to make you stay and listen to me, but I don't want to do that. You need to have your head straight, so you can wrap your brain around all the information I'm going to tell you. This is not a joke. Nor am I trying to fool you into what I'm here for. Which is you."

"What if I don't go with you, Sebastian? What then?"

He looked toward the ground and mumbled to himself. Then he raised his head with confidence and answered.

"As I told you before, I cannot go back without you. I'd have to stay here and I would die eventually. You know, whenever you deny me it hurts, in more ways than one. Almost like a punch to the stomach, but ten times worse. You've been doing that to me a lot lately."

I did not want to hurt him in any way. I was not the type to hurt anyone.

"I don't wish you pain, but you have to understand. Things like this do not happen everyday, and the things you've told me so far, are . . . are not making any sense. You do realize that?"

"Yes I do, Nyria, and I told you that the first time we talked . . . right?"

He was waiting for me to answer so he could continue.

"Yes, you did."

"OK then, I would like to finish. I am from a different realm and I am here to take you back with me. But I will not do anything until you are OK with *everything*. I just need you to understand and stop pushing me away."

I took a deep breath. The seriousness in his voice was really getting to me at this point. I knew this was not a joke and people holding cameras weren't going to jump out. I began to feel more comfortable in his presence.

Why? Probably because he had a new look to him now. He had a glow to him, almost like there was an aura around him.

"What is that around you? It looks like you're shining."

"You see it, Nyria?"

"Yes, I do."

He took a deep breath of relief.

"Finally! What you are seeing is my true self. This is how I see you. It is the connection making its form around us."

As he spoke, I felt this warm feeling surrounding me. Like I was closer to the sun. I glared at the light around us as it closed in on us.

"What's happening, Sebastian?"

"It's all right, Nyria, it won't hurt you, I promise. It's opening your mind to what I've been telling you. Can you feel the warmth of my heart within you yet?"

I had to think for a minute on what I was actually feeling. Something was warm, that's for sure. Was it really the warmth of his heart trying to tell me it's OK . . . or was this some type of magic trick I was now trapped in?

"All right, all right, I feel it. Now make it go away!"

Giggling, he replied, "It doesn't go away, Nyria. This is our connection. Every Newbian and their seed feel this for the rest of their lives."

Why did he always refer me as a seed?

"Sebastian, why do you call me your seed all the time? Is that all I am?"

He quickly answered in a soft tone. "No. This is what our elders called their creation. You are human, but when you go to Newbia you are born again in a different light. When people live and die here on Earth, there really is no purpose to their being. Most humans are created to keep Newbia from dying. We do grow old in Newbia, but your old is different to ours."

"Different?"

"Yes, different. You see, humans live until they're about eighty years old. Some can live until they're a little over the one hundred mark, but that is very uncommon. In Newbia, we live a lot longer. The oldest Newbian is 1,010 years old. He has another ten years before he is ready to die."

My eyes widened as my lips motioned the words, *Holy shit, that's crazy!*

"Wow, that's . . . sorry, I don't know what to say."

He smiled while keeping his head low. I didn't understand why he couldn't look me straight in the eye anymore. I wanted an answer. My curiosity was always getting the best of me lately.

"I know there's so much more for you to tell me, but let me ask you a question or two. Do you take me back with you right away? Will I be able to come back to Earth to see my friends and family, and do I become a Newbian right away or is there some type of ritual. And why do you hang your head low when you talk to me? Before you used to stare straight into my eyes. I get the feeling you're having trouble looking at me now. Is it the shine you see around me? Is it brighter than before?"

"Whoa, Nyria. Question or two, hey? Let me answer them before there's more."

He giggled as he replied.

"No, you don't go back to Newbia with me right away. We stay here until you feel comfortable enough to come back with me. Plus, children cannot be born there, so there is no rush . . ."

He paused while holding his index finger up toward me. I was about to interrupt him again.

"Just wait. Let me finish, Nyria. You cannot come back to Earth to visit anyone. Another human might get suspicious and find out about our realm. That would do more harm than good. Humans are not the most understanding people. They always need answers."

He waved a hand at me, indicating I was one of the not-so-understanding humans. I smiled because my actions lately were proof. I waited for him to answer my last question, but he just kept his head low, kicking the dirt under his feet.

"OK, what about my last question?"

He licked his lips and raised his head, taking a step toward me.

"Now that you see me as I've always seen you, I have a hard time controlling myself. The aura you're now seeing around us is pulling me in toward you. If I look straight into your eyes, I will try to . . ."

He paused.

My mouth was open and my eyes moved from side to side, waiting for him to continue.

But he didn't. He kept his head up while staring at me, moving closer and closer toward me. Like a lion stalking his prey.

What was happening?

"Block me, Nyria!" he shouted. "Block me!"

I had no idea what he was talking about. I took a few steps back as he approached me. The fence was now up against my back. I repeated over and over again in my head the word *block*. But he kept moving forward.

"Sebastian?"

He didn't reply, he just moved forward. He didn't seem to hear me say his name. My heart started to beat faster and faster.

What in the world is happening?

With one last try, I yelled his name.

"*Sebastian!*"

He lowered his head and fell to his knees. He was exhausted.

I wanted to move to his weak body as soon as he buckled over, but I was a little unsure.

His head pointing toward the ground, he said, "You have to learn to block me better than that, Nyria. If not, I might . . ."

Again he paused. Why couldn't he say it? What wasn't he telling me? And why was he so tired after . . . whatever just happened?

"Sebastian? Are you OK?"

I kept my distance, feeling concerned. He was trying to get up, but he seemed very weak. I felt bad, as if I had hurt him.

Maybe I did. What did I say? What did I do?

While I was arguing with myself in my head, he got up to his feet, keeping his head low.

"I'm all right. I just need a few minutes."

He took a deep breath in and out. I was puzzled, and curiosity bit again. Now that he was back to his feet I took a brave step toward him with my hand out. Maybe to help him or push him away if I felt uneasy. I wasn't sure which; nonetheless, I was moving forward.

The concern of him hurting me was gone. Now I had sympathy and desire.

Getting to his feet, he wiped away the dirt from his knees.

"I didn't think this would have happen so quickly. Usually takes a month or two, but . . ."

He gasped.

"What? What just happened, Sebastian? What usually takes a month?"

Kids were now outside running toward the park. I knew we couldn't let others know about him or why he was here. Plus, he was still a bit weak.

Why I said this I have no idea, but it came out and I didn't regret it even after I said it.

"Come on, we can't keep talking here. Someone will hear us or see you doing . . . whatever it was you were doing."

He looked up at me baffled.

"Where are we going to go?"

The words seem to fall off my lips as if I wanted to say them all along.

"Back to my place, where we can talk openly without having an audience."

I could tell he liked this idea. His pearly whites were showing.

Walking back to my apartment, I noticed we were side by side, with no more distance between us. I didn't want to think about it, so I kept asking him if he was OK. He assured me he was fine, but he wasn't walking as fast as he usually did.

When we reached my building doors, I grabbed my keys out my pocket and opened the door. He held it for me to go in first, as a gentleman would.

As I walked in, I looked back at him, noticing him admiring my ass.

"Do you mind?"

"Sorry."

Now standing in front of my apartment door, hesitation began.

"It's OK, Nyria, it's all good."

I opened the door and waved him in. He stood there with his big blue eyes waiting for me to walk in first.

Quickly I darted in. I heard my landlord whistling on the other side of the corridor, walking toward my end of the hallway. I didn't want him to stop and talk to me. He was very annoying and long-winded.

Sebastian noticed me move quickly, so he followed.

I closed the door behind him and leaned against it.

"Please, have a seat. Do you want something to drink?"

"Yes, please . . . water would be good."

I strolled to the fridge and grabbed a bottle of water. I entered the living room and sat on the chair adjacent to his.

"Why did you fall to your knees? What happened back there?"

He took a mouthful of water before be began.

"I don't know how to say this without you taking it the wrong way, but . . . since we've made our connection again and you see me as I've always seen you, my body is craving you. This is strange, because it usually doesn't happen until we've been together for a month or two. Looking straight into your eyes makes me want to . . ."

Again he paused.

"Just say it. I promise I won't go crazy."

I giggled, realizing this was why he was having a hard time telling me what was on his mind.

He smiled and laughed to himself before continuing.

"After meeting, our seeds . . . I mean, our *creations*, our hormones come into play. I cannot look you straight in the eyes for a long period of time without wanting to make love to you. It's a chemical reaction between our two bodies that is usually felt by the Newbian man first. Eventually, you'll feel it too. You need to block me so I don't advance on you whenever you don't want me to feel this way. It hurts me, but not as bad as when you deny me. It's not as painful. Then the feeling goes away."

"Wait, you're saying if you stare at me for even five seconds, you'll want to . . . have sex with me?"

"Not sex, Nyria, that is something humans do whenever they want to get their jollies. Newbians make love . . . some more aggressive than others, but it's lovemaking, not just sex."

"Oh. And if I don't block you, what then?"

I wanted to know the answer. He gripped the water bottle slightly.

"Are you asking me . . . if you don't want to make love and I do . . . and you don't block me, what would happen?"

"Yes."

"Well, I would become overpowering . . . still making love, just without your permission. If you wanted to make love, that's a different story."

He looked up at me then back to the floor, and rubbed the carpet with his socked feet.

"Alrighty then. I thought you said there's no chaos or hate in your world? That's rape, you know?"

He quickly responded with a bit of sharpness in his voice.

"That's not hate, chaos or rape, Nyria. It's a chemical reaction that we have no control over. That is why you need to learn to block me whenever I stare into your eyes. Or else I will have to walk around with my head down while I am with you. It's not to hurt you. It's something we Newbians have no control over, no matter if you're on Earth or in Newbia. Which I think is pointless, because making love anywhere should always result in having children."

I knew the children thing was a touchy subject, so I changed the topic.

"Well, if you're gonna be sticking around here, you're going to have to teach me how to block you. Oh yeah, one more thing. Can you hear me if I talk in my own head or can I only hear your voice in my head?"

"I love how you ask questions, Nyria, they come from nowhere. We can talk to each other through thought. I know what you are thinking and I can respond. You cannot, on the other hand. I can relay a message, but, that's it. Why do you ask?"

"Just wondering."

There was a motive behind that question—the time I yelled at him in my mind to get him out of my head and he didn't hear me.

Or did he? Hmmm, interesting . . .

"Is there more I need to know?"

He took another gulp off water before standing up.

"Yes, but I'm feeling a little tired. I must sleep to get my energy back. I only need a few hours of sleep, so I will come back later to tell you the rest."

"Where are you going?"

"Home."

"Home? How? I thought you said you cannot go back without me?"

He shook his head and laughed again.

"I am allowed to go home to sleep, but not to stay. I have to come back here each day to tell you about Newbia and your purpose, in hopes that eventually you'll come back with me forever."

"Yes, but how do you go home and how do you come back to Earth each time?"

This should be interesting, I thought. He washed down the rest of the water and placed the bottle on my coffee table.

"I will show you, but you cannot follow me, OK? Ok, Nyria?"

"OK. Um, what do you mean follow you?"

Taking a few steps toward my balcony doors, he turned to face me. I stood up.

"I will open my realm and walk through. It is left open for ten seconds afterwards. This is what I meant by don't follow me. I don't know what would happen if you did. The elders tells us to make sure our seeds . . . creations are aware of this rule. Unless they are coming back with us forever."

My eyes grew wide.

"I see. Well, I won't follow you, I can promise you that. I've had enough of the unknown for one day. When will I see you again?"

I stuttered as I moved in a bit closer.

"Tomorrow is Sunday and I know you don't have to work. You usually get up around 8:00 a.m. I know this because I'm awake when you are. I will give you an hour before I come. Is that enough time, or do you—"

I interrupted him. "No, that's fine."

Smiling, he walked toward me. Gracefully, he took my face in his hands and stared into my eyes.

"Block me so I can say this, please."

I closed my eyes, trying to block him. Meanwhile, he broke into a laugh.

I opened my eyes quickly to see why he was laughing. Still holding my face in his warm grip, he softly chuckled.

"Don't close your eyes. It doesn't work like that, Nyria."

I started to giggle as well.

Staring deep into his beautiful blue eyes, I began to get the idea of how to block him.

I'm doing it! a voice yelled in my head.

He licked his lips then gently uttered, "Thank you for listening to me, Nyria. I'm glad to have you as my creation. Your stubbornness and dynamics intrigue me. You're different, and I like that. You're not just an average girl as you see yourself. You're beautiful in more ways than one. I wouldn't change you for anything. I know this might sound over the top, but I've loved you since the day you were born. And now my love seems to have taken a deeper meaning."

He smiled as tears fell from his eyes. I too had tears filling my eye sockets.

Hearing someone say those things to me were overwhelming. I felt the truth behind all that he said.

Was it the aura or was it really his heart in mine?

"Goodnight, Nyria, I'll see you tomorrow. Sleep peacefully."

I was biting my bottom lip as he spoke. He licked his lips one last time before he placed them on mine.

It felt like we were kissing forever, but it was just for a second or two.

My eyes stayed closed. I didn't want to open them. It felt like a dream I didn't want to wake up from.

I felt the heat coming for his face and the wetness of his tongue touching mine. Then cool air came between us.

We were not kissing anymore. His face was apart from mine. I still had my lips in a kissing position. All the while, he smiled at me.

He kissed my forehead and removed his hands from my face. He took a step back and said, "Goodnight."

He reached out to put his hand on the balcony doors, and the glass became wavy, like boiling water. He turned to walk through it.

But before he did, he took one last look at me and winked. Then he was gone.

His Return

I walked over to the balcony doors, fascinated by the wavy glass. I wanted to touch it, but he had told me not to follow. My hand seemed to have a mind of its own, because I began to reach for it.

As soon as my fingertips reached the glass, the waviness disappeared. It looked normal again.

"This has to be a dream, and I haven't woken up from it yet."

I shook my head, headed for my bedroom. I lay there thinking of him.

I made sure I set my alarm clock for 8 a.m. to give me enough time to freshen up. Falling asleep wasn't an issue.

The next thing I heard was *beep, beep, beep!* I hit the snooze button, swung the blankets off of me and hurried to the shower to wash up.

Spending only ten minutes to wash up, I went to the living room and waited for him to return.

It was now 8 a.m. and he still wasn't here.

Where is he? Just then my buzzer rang. I ran to let him in the building doors.

Pacing back and forth, waiting for him to knock at my door, I opened it impatiently to find Scott walking down the hall.

"Uh oh," I whispered.

I smiled at Scott as he approached. He gave me a big hug and kiss on the cheek.

"Hey girly, looking good!"

"Thanks dude, right back atcha. What are you doing here?"

"Nice to see you too, Nyria. Geez. I can't stop by and see how my best friend is doing? Since she doesn't call me anymore."

I folded my arms across my chest in defence and told him to come in. Before I could say another word my buzzer rang again.

It's him, Sebastian.

I hesitated for a second. Scott was eyeballing me, waiting for me to let the person in the building.

"Are you going to get that, Nyria?"

I went to the buzzer slowly, bringing my finger up to the button. Scott's face showed he was more confused than ever.

"You OK, chick?"

"Yeah, I'm fine. Why?"

Scott looked at me with seriousness written all over his face.

"'Cause you're acting really weird. More than normal, I might add."

Before I could respond, there was a knock at my door. Scott dashed to open it to see what I was so weirded out about.

"Hello, can I help you?" Scott announced.

Sebastian stepped back in shock. I went to pull the door fully open so he could see me.

"Hi. Don't mind him, he's the watchdog, as you can tell."

I snickered as I waved Sebastian in. As he entered, I noticed the two of them locked in a staring competition.

"OK. Um, Scott, Sebastian. Sebastian, Scott."

Scott didn't put his hand out to greet Sebastian's. He stood with his hands in fists.

"Yeah, nice to meet you, buddy," Scott stated.

"Nice to meet you too," Sebastian answered.

There was absolutely nothing nice about this meeting.

I came between them, feeling the heat in the room coming from Scott's stance.

"Scott was just leaving, weren't you, Scott?" I said with a little aggression in my voice.

"No, I think I'll stay, thank you very much." He sat on my sofa.

Sebastian laughed under his breath so no one would hear. I stood there frozen in thought. How am I supposed to describe how I met Sebastian? I knew Scott was going to ask eventually.

Gently, I took hold of Sebastian's arm and asked him to sit. He smiled at me while asking, "Did you have a good sleep?"

I didn't even fully hear Sebastian after he said the word *have*, because Scott interrupted him.

"You were with this guy last night?"

I looked at Scott and he knew I was angry at his ignorance.

"What?" Scott counteracted to my defensive posture.

"Can I talk to you for a moment, Scott?"

I walked into the kitchen with Scott on my heels. I turned to him and said in a low whisper, "OK, you're not my dad, remember, and you're not being nice. He's a friend of mine and I'd appreciate—"

"A friend? I've never heard nor seen this Joey before."

"Listen, shithead, I don't tell you everything because you're so overprotective. I knew you'd go stupid for some odd reason. But seriously, can I call you later? I'll tell you all about it."

"No, you can tell me now. You were hiding this Joey from me for some reason and now I wanna know why."

"First of all, his name is Sebastian, so drop the Joey, OK? Secondly, I'm a grown woman who doesn't have to answer to you. I'm so pissed off at you right now. I think it's best you leave."

I pointed to the door, motioning Scott's dismissal, and Sebastian stood behind me with anger in his eyes. I could feel him getting upset. I could feel his emotions coming from inside me. I knew what he was feeling.

I didn't have to look back to see if he was standing there, because Scott's eyes were focused on him.

"What? Mind your business, buddy. Go sit back down."

Sebastian didn't move. He looked as if he were about to remove Scott himself. I screamed at the top of my lungs, "Scott! Stop being an ass and leave, *now*! He's my friend, and I've never treated any of your friends like this."

Sebastian still stood behind me. I felt his hands move across my back, about to move me out of the way gracefully. He was about to remove Scott from my apartment when Scott finally agreed.

"Fine, I'm outta here. Call me when your pretty boy leaves."

He nudged Sebastian as he walked by. Sebastian didn't move; he was still as a brick wall, and Scott hurt himself when he shoved into his shoulder. I could see it on his face. He grabbed his shoulder while walking out my door and slammed it shut. I put my face in the palms of my hands.

"I'm so sorry. He's always like that when he sees me with another guy."

Sebastian removed my hands from my face.

"That's because he loves you."

I looked at him, startled.

"No, no way, he's like a big brother to me. He doesn't look at me like that."

Sebastian laughed.

"Guys only act like that when they want something and someone else moves in on their territory."

"No, you got it all wrong. You see, I had a rough time with my ex-boyfriend a year ago and Scott hated him because he was abusive to me. Scott kept telling me to leave him, but I never listen. Since then, *all* guys are a threat. He will never change unless shown otherwise, I hope. I love the asshole. He's always been there for me when I needed him the most. He'll be this way until the day he dies."

"Hmmm."

"Why the hmmm?"

"Nothing. I just don't see it that way, that's all. But you love him and I respect that."

I moseyed toward the cupboard to find something to eat, and I felt him up against my back.

"You're hungry, aren't you? I know because you're making my belly grumble."

He rubbed my stomach from behind. I swiftly moved from his approach and questioned him.

"You feel what I feel too?"

"Yes. I ate but I can tell you're hungry. I told you before, we have a lot in common. I felt you until you turned eighteen, remember me telling you that?"

"Yes, but how do you . . ."

I didn't finish because I didn't know what to ask, exactly. He smiled at me, all the while hanging his head low.

"Since our connection at the park, we can feel each other's emotions. Did you feel mine when your friend Scott was here?"

I thought for a moment and said, "Yeah, I did, but I just thought . . . I don't know what I thought."

Shaking his head, he headed toward my cupboards.

"Here, let me get you something to eat. I love to cook. Plus, I'm very good at it."

Sebastian was looking through my cupboards, almost as if he had been here before. He knew where everything was.

I didn't ask because I already knew the answer. I think.

He made hash browns, eggs and bacon. It tasted as good as it looked.

"Thank you. That's awesome you can cook."

"You're welcome. There's more where that came from."

Walking out of the kitchen, I started picking my teeth.

"I need to brush my teeth, I'll be right back."

I went into the washroom to clean my teeth and any other food left on my face. I heard water running.

By the time I was finished, I saw Sebastian standing at the entrance of the kitchen waiting for me to join him. I went in and peeked at the dishes that were washed and sitting to dry.

"You didn't have to do my dishes too."

"I know. Now you don't have to worry about them. We need to talk."

I felt comfortable with him, so he had my full attention.

BOOM!

I jumped in the air.

"What was that?" I yelled, scared half to death.

He grinned.

"Rain. We're supposed to get the tail end of a hurricane today. Don't you watch your weather channel?"

"To be honest, I don't watch much TV, so no, I didn't. Is it supposed to get bad outside?"

I opened the curtains to see blackness covering the sky, bolts of light flashing over it.

He was now standing beside me, looking out the window as well.

"This is amazing from my realm. Looking down at Earth from a distance, seeing it covered in clouds is very beautiful in its own way."

"You can see Earth from Newbia?"

"Yes, but Earth is in a different realm. Newbia is beside it. It almost looks like watching a pot full of water. You'll see."

"I will? You're sure about that, huh?"

He turned his face toward me and stared straight into my eyes, answering with a strong and confident tone, "Yes. I'm sure."

His eyes seem to have taken on a different colour today. They were now aqua.

"Your eyes, they're . . ."

I didn't finish my sentence. Something changed. He had that lion-stalking-prey thingy happening again. Only this time he didn't tell me to block him. I couldn't look away.

Why? What was happening? Was he controlling me?

No, he wouldn't do that. Or would he?

I fought to block him. He moved forward, taking hold of my waist, breathing very heavy. I was trapped in his eyes and a part of me didn't want to get out. But lovemaking at this point wasn't on my agenda.

There was so much to learn, so much to talk about. Plus, I hadnb't known him long enough to have him inside of me.

His hands were now gripping my waist harder and harder. He wasn't hurting me, but he was dominating the situation.

I couldn't talk or move at this point. I knew what was happening. I could feel his body against mine.

His lower half was now poking me through his jeans and his face grew closer.

He licked his bottom lip. In that instant, we were kissing. In one powerful motion I was lifted off the ground.

Wrapping my legs around his waist, I felt myself enjoying this. Nothing else was on my mind but him.

Like a bird flying free in the sky we entered my bedroom, where he laid me down with my legs around his waist.

He started kissing my neck, biting me gently as he removed my top. Then my shorts, along with my underwear that he seemed to have grabbed while taking my shorts off.

The only thing left on my body was a green laced bra that I bought at La Senza a year ago.

"You're mine," he whispered in my ear while biting my earlobe.

Moaning from his touch and the whispers in my ear, he kept speaking in a soft low tone. kissing and touching me ever so carefully. My hands ran through his short blond hair.

Caught in the moment, I reached down to unbuckle his jeans. He slipped them off in one motion. No sooner did that happen than he thrust himself in me. In return I let out a loud moan of pleasure.

Colours filled the room as he made love to me like I've never been made love to before.

He was powerful but gentle until I started biting his chest. He became more aggressive, dominating me.

The feeling was overwhelming. The more I called his name, the more passion came from him.

Near the end both of us were lifted off the bed by a force unknown to man. An explosion took place.

I was in another world. Not Newbia, not Earth, but our own.

Together

I turned over and felt a body lying next to me. I felt numb from head to toe. Bodystoned.

I opened my eyes to find Sebastian sprawled with his arms above his head.

"Oh my god, what did I do?" I asked myself as I slowly crept out of the bed.

"Good morning, Nyria"

I sat straight up. My eyes widened as I heard him say my name.

"Good . . . good morning"

He noticed that my voice was off a little and he felt my emotions flowing through me. He knew I was surprised and a little upset.

"You're not upset, are you, Nyria?"

"No, I just . . . I remember everything, but what happened? How did we end up making love?"

He came closer to me and put his hands on my shoulders.

"It was my fault."

"Your fault? Did you trick me? No, let me guess: you were controlling me, weren't you?"

He sat up with me. "No! No. I would never do that. I just stared in your eyes and I wanted you. You didn't block me. I can't control what happens after that. You have the power to stop me . . . and only you."

His hands dropped from my shoulders as he climbed out of bed. His body looked muscular and strong. I could see every detail. Smooth but rough at the same time.

"I will leave. I see you're not feeling the same as I am right now."

I waited for a second to respond. I wanted to see if I could patch in to his feelings.

There they were. Loving, careful, sincere and genuine . . .

"Sebastian, I'm sorry. I just . . . I hardly know you and things are . . . how should I say this . . . not normal. Our situation is out of this world. It's not your fault. Please don't go. I'm not mad or anything, just very confused. I don't do this type of thing, where I sleep with someone I hardly know, especially someone like you. Oh shit . . . that came out wrong."

"I know what you mean, Nyria, it's fine. How about I go and come back when you're not so confused. There's so much more to talk about."

"Sebastian, I know I'm making you feel uncomfortable. I sense it. You have to remember I can feel your feelings too. So don't lie to me."

He crossed his arms over his chest.

"I'm not lying, I just don't want to upset you, that's all."

"Well, I have to get ready for work, so . . ."

"Yeah, I'm going to take my car in for an inspection. A mechanic said it's almost due. I don't understand why you humans do that every year. I guess it's for safety reasons."

"That's right, you have a BMW. Where is it, anyway? You don't take it with you when you go back to Newbia, do you?"

"No, I leave the car at a storage facility whenever I'm not using it. They don't charge very much, either."

I was taking his mind off the awkward conversation we just had.

As he was putting on his jeans that were at the end of my bed, I got up and headed to the shower. He watched me walk out of the room. I could feel his eyes on me. His emotions were going crazy.

"You like what you see, huh?"

He smiled but kept his head low. He didn't want a re-enactment of the previous night.

As I climbed in the shower, he poked his head in the bathroom and asked if he could use the toilet.

"Sure, just don't flush or the water will change."

"OK. I will." He chuckled out loud.

"Sebastian, I know you want to fill me in on all the other stuff. How about you meet me after work so we can finish talking?"

"Sounds good."

I heard him zipper his jeans. I knew he was done.

"I'm going to go, Nyria. I will see you after your shift, OK?"

He pulled the shower curtain back and his beautiful face appeared. My hands were full of soap, so he pulled my face toward his and said, "Sorry about last night. I—"

I cut him off right away.

"Please stop apologizing for that. I enjoyed all of it. I have never had anyone make me feel like that before. And—"

He interrupted me.

"Neither did I. That was the first time for me."

I was shocked at his response. I was his first? That makes sense. I'm his seed— I mean, creation.

Now I was feeling bad for being upset when he was so happy.

"Nyria, I just wanted to say I'm happy, and I know this probably doesn't sit well with you yet, but I love you."

My eyes were full of tears. I fought to keep them back. I knew he felt what I was feeling.

"OK, thanks."

Closing the curtain behind him, I stood there without knowing what to feel or say.

By the time I rinsed my hands off and opened the curtain he was gone.

I hurried into work that morning, late as usual. Karen was always good to me.

"Good morning, Nyria," Karen said from her office.

"Good morning, Karen."

I poked my head in just to have her smile at me.

"How was your weekend, darling?" she asked.

"It was good. And yours?"

I knew she had lots to tell me. She had a new boyfriend, six years younger than her. She would be turning fifty-six soon. She never wanted anyone to know her age, but she felt comfortable with me.

The day of her daughter's funeral, she cried in my arms, saying, "I'm burying my daughter. Who would have thought. Children are supposed to bury their parents. I'm divorced and I'm fifty-four years old, who would marry me now?"

I remembered the words because she kept saying them over and over again. Two years have passed and I remember it like it was yesterday. Now she seemed so happy with her new man. I was very happy for her and I loved hearing her stories. She was so cheerful when I asked how her weekend was. She came skipping out of her office with a big smile on her face.

"Ben asked me to marry him. Can you believe that?"

"Yes, I can. You're a wonderful woman, Karen, and you have so much love to give. I'm not surprised he asked you. Congratulations."

She pranced over to me and gave me the biggest hug ever.

"OK, dinner is about to open, wanna grab me the chalkboard so I can put the daily specials on it?"

"No problem."

I went to the front of the store. A young man was peering in the window at me. His smile was wide and his hair was a little messy. I quickly went back to give Karen the chalkboard.

"Thanks, Nyria. OK honey, go start the coffee maker. Bev called and she is running a little late, so it's all you until she arrives."

I went back to the front of the diner. The young man was still peering in at me. He waved at me vigorously. I waved back, and gave him half a smile.

I started the coffee maker. The boys in the back were starting to cook. I could smell the bacon frying.

Karen walked through proudly and opened the diner's doors.

"Oh, by the way, I hired another girl. She should be here any minute. Can you show her the ropes, Nyria?"

"Sure."

People started coming in and taking seats. Most of them sat in their usual spots. The young man who had been peering in at me through the big picture window sat at the counter stool. He was turning it around and around, trying to get my attention.

A young girl walked in and approached me, introducing herself as Kim the new waitress.

"Oh, um, hi. We were waiting for you. You can put your things in the back room. There are lockers back there too. Pick one. Then come back out I will show you everything you need to know."

Bev walked through the doors.

"Hi, my name is Bev. I'll show you where to put your things," she told the young girl, giving me a dirty look. I never really knew why she hated me so much. Probably because people liked me more than her. She had a bad attitude and it showed.

I continued doing my rounds with each table, taking orders and placing them. I noticed Bev standing with Kim, showing her where things were.

The young man sitting at the counter was turned all the way around facing me. He coughed, trying to get my attention.

Bev quickly saw him and moved in.

"Hi, I'm Bev. Can I get you something to drink?"

Turning his stool toward her, he looked her up and down with a disgusted frown.

"No thanks. I'm waiting for her," he said, pointing at me.

"Pfff!" she replied. She went to greet the other customers, Kim trailing behind her like a lost puppy.

As I walked around the counter to place another order, the young man *pssst* at me.

"Hi, I'm Adam."

"Hi, sorry about that. What can I get you?"

"What's good? Besides you."

I laughed out loud, but caught myself. That was rude, I thought.

"Um, today's special is bacon and eggs with fried mushrooms for $2.99. It's pretty good."

"OK, I'll have that, please."

As I wrote his order on my pad, he leaned toward me and whispered, "While you're at it, write your number down too."

What was with guys lately? I have one from a different realm and this knucklehead in front of me.

"Yeah, right," I smirked.

Walking away to take other orders, I felt his eyes all over me. Yuck.

"Excuse me, miss," someone called out. I looked back to see who he was talking to. A man was holding a dozen roses of all colours and a big balloon that read, "You're my dream."

"Me?" I asked.

"I don't know. Are you Nyria?"

"Yes, I am."

"Then yup, this is for you, dear."

I took the roses in my arms. The balloon was attached to them. The man walked away saying, "Someone has the hots for you, darling."

"Yeah, thanks." But who?

Bev, Karen, Kim and all the customers were staring at me.

"Open it, dear!" someone yelled out from across the diner.

I placed the roses on the counter and opened the card. It read:

You are the sun that keeps me warm.
The moon that shines for me at night
and the beat within my heart.
Have a beautiful day, gorgeous.
Sebastian

My mind went blank. My heart dropped to the bottom of my stomach. Could it be true? Did I love him? I've only known him for four days.

"So? Who sent them?" Karen asked, standing beside me trying to read the card.

"I don't kiss and tell," I replied, sliding away from her and hiding the card under my chin.

Someone yelled out, "It's a secret admirer, I bet."

Giggles swarmed through the diner.

"OK, ladies, back to work. Nyria, put them out back, sweetie," Karen advised me.

I picked the roses up off the counter and held them close to my chest as I walked out back to place them on Karen's desk. I knew this was the best place to put them so no one would ruin them. Bev would be the first one to rip them up. Bitch.

Back to work, I said to myself.

Happy as a clam, I grabbed the food that was waiting for table one. I took their food to them with a big smile on my face.

"Nice flowers, dear," a construction worker said as I put his food in front of him.

"Thank you."

The young man that introduced himself as Adam was obviously upset. His fist was planted on the counter as though he were about to punch someone. He jumped to his feet and stormed out the door.

What was that all about? He didn't even get his order yet.

"Jim! Cancel that special for the counter. He just left."

I yelled back to the cook.

"'Kay," he replied.

That was weird. I wonder why he stormed out of here?

I went back to work as if nothing had happened. Time flew by, especially with the new girl on the floor. Bev was busy training her and taking orders. Good, she was out of my hair for once. I didn't even take a break that day, it was that busy. The whole day, he was on my mind. I couldn't stop thinking about him and how he made me feel the night before. It was magical. I must have had five orgasms.

Was I falling in love with him?

"Nyria? Do you wanna work overtime or what? It's six o'clock," Karen sang out.

I looked at the clock hanging just above the coffee maker.

"No, I'm gone like last night's dinner," I bellowed back, being a smart-ass.

She smiled and said, "Make sure you grab your flowers. Oh, and your tips."

"Oh, I won't forget them."

Darting back to Karen's office I grabbed my tip jar and roses. I was eager to see Sebastian. I threw my clothes into my locker and headed for the front doors.

"'Night Karen, I'm off tomorrow. See you Wednesday."

"'Night, baby."

I opened the front doors and he was there waiting for me, leaning against his 1996 BMW and smiling. I jogged to him and threw myself into his arms, squeezing him and whispering, "You're such a sweetheart. Thank you. You made my day. I'm so sorry about this morning. Please forgive me. I was an ass."

He placed his finger over my lips and said, "I will do whatever it is that makes you happy. When you're happy, I'm happy. I love seeing your face light up along with the shine that's already there. Plus, I love you."

My eyes met his. I wanted him to take me right there and make passionate love to me, but he lowered his head.

I placed my hand under his chin to see his big blue eyes.

"You don't need to look away anymore. I can block you, I'm sure of it. I love seeing your eyes; they're beautiful just as you are. You know what?"

"What, Nyria?"

I paused and stared deep into his eyes. "I love you too."

He held me tighter in his arms and swung me around, kissing me all over my neck. He was ecstatic.

I felt the same way.

Maybe now it wouldn't be so hard for me to listen and understand all that he had to tell me.

He gazed into my eyes while saying, "Let's get out of here. Let's go home where I can spoil you. I'll cook supper and give you the best back rub you've ever had."

"That sounds great."

Still in his grip, I was carried to the passenger-side door while he kissed me. He put me down gently and opened the car door. I plopped in and heard a horn.

Who's that? I turned in my seat . . . Scott.

I climbed out of the car to greet him. I hoped he wasn't going to make a fool out of me in front of my job.

"Hey babe. Pretty boy driving you home, I see."

"Stop it, Scott."

He sprung out of his car and strutted toward Sebastian.

"Hey," he nodded.

I stood by the both of them to make sure nothing happened. I felt Sebastian's blood boil.

Scott reached out his hand to Sebastian.

"Sorry about the other day. It's just that . . . she's my girl. I mean, she's my little sis and I love her and I want to be sure she's . . . you know."

Sebastian understood. I felt his blood pressure level come down to normal again. He took Scott's hand in a firm grip.

"You have no worries. She's in good hands, I can promise you that."

Excitement filled my veins as my two favourite guys made amends. Smiling at Scott, I threw my arms around him and whispered, "Thank you. I love you too, ya jerk."

I gave him a kiss on the cheek as I let him go.

"Well, I see you got a ride home, so I'm gonna be going."

"I'll give you a call later, Scott."

"OK babe. But I'm going to Truro tomorrow, so how's about I call you when I come back?"

I forgot he had a training in Truro that week.

"OK Scott, sounds good. Safe trip, all right?"

He gave me a salute and nodded at Sebastian, who waved in return.

Scott sped off like he was racing Dale Earnhardt Jr.

I climbed back into the car with Sebastian and we headed for home.

When we arrived, I threw my clothes off and bounced into the shower. As I was drying off I found Sebastian cooking a lobster dinner. My favourite.

"How'd you know?"

"It's my favourite too."

While the lobster cooked, I leaped on top of the counter and slid him between my thighs.

"Something weird happen to me today."

"Yeah? What?"

"A young man came into the diner. He ordered, then got upset when my flowers came—which I loved, by the way—and he took off out the door without eating or paying for his food. But before that . . . he was peeking at me through the big picture window before the store was even open. He called himself Adam."

Sebastian shook his head and suggested that some humans are weirder than others, and laughed between each word.

"Don't worry about him. He probably came from the Nova Scotia Mental Hospital."

I started laughing. Not at what he said but, but at the way he found it so funny.

The lobster was done. We sat down at my little round table and ate while we laughed and chatted.

"OK, I'm ready to hear about Newbia again."

He sat back in his chair and started from where he had left off. Before he continued his story, I asked him a question.

"Haven't you noticed something?"

"What?"

He looked around the room to see if I had changed something.

"No, not the room. The fact that you are looking me straight in the eye. I am blocking you without trying. I've got it!"

"Yeah, I did notice. I just didn't say anything because if you try too hard sometimes it can backfire," he added with a smirk on his face. His eyes started to turn colours again, blue to aqua.

"Sebastian?" I said his name over and over again. Eventually, I knew I'd have to give up, because he was right. It was backfiring.

Oh, why not? I thought.

"Come and get me," I teased him as I got up from the table and stared deep into his eyes.

There's always tomorrow to learn more about Newbia, I thought.

There was no turning back now. He had me in his grip.

The Story

My body felt stiff as I rolled over, waking up. I heard the birds chirping. I knew he would be up soon.

We were connected to the point that whenever my eyes opened, so did his.

"Good morning, Sebastian," I whispered in his ear.

"Good morning, Nyria. How was your sleep?"

"I slept like a baby."

I must have fallen asleep right after we made love, because everything after that is a blur. I reached over him to move my alarm clock to see what time it was.

9:33 a.m.

I flopped back to my side, then decided to get up to shower.

"Do you want to join, Sebastian?"

He threw the blankets off, indicating he was ready and willing to join me. Together we went to the bathroom. He slapped my ass as we walked in. I was the first to get in the shower. After using the washroom, he climbed in with a grin on his face.

We stayed in the shower for about thirty minutes, holding each other as the water trickled down our backs.

"Are you hungry, Nyria? I'll make breakfast."

"You know I am."

I giggled.

He washed up and was the first one out the bathroom. I took a little longer than he did. I wanted to shave my legs.

By the time I was dried up and dressed he had breakfast on the table. He sat in the chair that faced the hallway so he could see me coming.

I sat down and smiled at him, so enlightened by his grace. He glowed more than usual. I knew my heart was a part of his now.

"I'm ready to hear more about Newbia."

His eyes were shining as he felt my interest intensify. I wanted to know more about his unknown realm.

"How about you turn your phone off so there's no interruptions?"

I agreed, and stood up to shut it off. I sat on the sofa and he came in to join me, wrapping me into his arms. He began to tell me about the beautiful realm I was soon to belong to.

"Newbia is one of the first realms to exist. The other realm is called Lubria. It is well known to humans; you call it a galaxy. People in Lubria are very intelligent and they have an unmistakable appearance. You call them aliens, I believe. Well, they're called Lubrians. The only difference from them to us is that we do not take humans to experiment on. We take your kind to keep our people and realm alive. Lubrians can reproduce in their realm, we cannot.

"We used to be able to have children, but we went to war with Lubria millions of years ago. They took all of our woman for experiments. Why, we do not know. And now, the woman are sterile.

"They also left something in our atmosphere that's keeping woman from having children. But one woman was left untainted. Her name was Zealous. She reproduced with all of the men in Newbia over several thousands of years, just so her people could live on.

"Her first two children were Karah and Lyzaic. They were the first Newbian seeds placed on Earth. They lived a hundred years after they arrived, and had multiple children. We could not keep them hidden in Newbia. We were trying to keep them a secret from the Lubrians.

"So that is why Earth was created in the Lubrian realm. The reason for this is . . . well, let's just say, we tried to outsmart them by hiding Earth in their own realm. Their universe is much bigger than ours. We thought they would never think to look in their own backyard.

"Eventually, they found our creation. They travel to Earth to do experiments. That's why you hear about abductions once in a while. It's true. Soon, Earth's women will be sterile, just like the woman in Newbia. Hopefully, one day a woman like Zealous will enter our realm and be able to reproduce again.

"Oh, and about the Lubrians: they are curious creatures that want to know everything. They want everything to be theirs. They're selfish.-We don't really know why they are so hell-bent on knowing everything. In any case, we live side by side now without any wars. Don't get me wrong, Newbia still has warriors to defend it. That's if the Lubrians decide to make war against us again.

"Warriors are usually men unable to reproduce, or men who have come back to Newbia after they have found their seeds. We despise war or any type of aggression. But there's one exception: if you go to Earth and kill someone, the penalty is death. As soon as you return to Newbia, death will follow. We cannot kill our own creations. For you are what keep us alive. There aren't many rules that dominate our people, but murder is not tolerated.

"We all need balance. This is how we keep peace. We live as we wish. We want nothing but good in our realm. And if you go against that, you become our enemy. Barbaric behaviour must be demolished. I know it seems harsh, but this is how we keep peace.

"There are Newbian elders we answers to. They are the oldest of our people. When each of them die, the next in line will take their place.

"Ok, I'm getting sidetracked. Where was I? Oh, right . . . every twenty-six years Newbian men come to Earth to find their seeds. We impregnate them on Earth and then bring them back to Newbia. Once you come to Newbia, you can no longer bear children, this is why we wait until the children are born here on Earth. When a Newbian is born, their seed is born too. This is how we are connected. We are given life at the same time. Our feelings and thoughts go hand and hand. We fall in love with our seeds the day we are born. We feel it as if it was natural. When you were born, Nyria, I was too. But my parents, Bruce and Charlene, took me to Newbia where I grew up. I felt and knew you until we were eighteen years old. Something changed. The elders could not explain why it happened. So they did a lot of tests on me for six years, thinking it was a chemical imbalance on my part. When they found nothing out of the ordinary, they told me to go to Earth to find you.

"Even though Newbian men only come to Earth when they are twenty-six years old, my elders wanted me to find you two years earlier, just to make sure things are as they should be. When I first came to Earth I didn't find you right away, but eventually I did. Obviously. I only go back to Newbia to sleep, as I told you before.

"The elders always meet with me before I return to Earth, to talk to me about you. To see if something was wrong in our connection. I didn't give them many answers, because I am still not sure there is even a problem. I told them I think that you and I are the first to experience the disconnection our kind might be facing in the years to come. They too believe this. Something has changed and we don't know what it is. We are just hopeful that it's something for the better.

"Oh yeah . . . how we keep humans from knowing about us and what we do . . .

"Well, when our seeds return to Newbia with us, the minds of friends and families are wiped of any memory they have of you.

It's like you never existed. We cannot take the chance of anyone finding out about us, because humans are just like the Lubrians. They will experiment on us. Or even worse, they might kill us. We cannot take that chance. Newbians will protect their seeds at any cost, even if it means death when we return to Newbia. Our seeds are the key for our survival. Without you we would die. Newbians need to keep your kind alive.

"Not all humans are brought back to Newbia. There are more humans than Newbians. Some Newbians say there's a legend about our realm changing, but the elders will not allow us to speak of it. They are unsure it will come true. I hope it's something better for our realm. But again, I don't even know what this legend is . . . yet."

He took a deep breath and unwrapped his arms that held me close to him. He got up and headed for the kitchen. I heard the fridge open then close. He came back with a bottle of water.

After opening it, he drank the whole thing in one glop.

"Sorry, I didn't mean to go on and on. I just want you to know everything. Wow . . . my mouth was dry."

My mind was going a mile a minute. I had taken so much information in I was in overload mode. I just stared at him.

"Nyria, you OK?"

"Yes, I'm fine, Sebastian. That was a lot of info . . . I'm just lost for words. I understand everything now. But I'm not ready nor willing to leave yet."

"I know. I'm not asking you to pack up and leave right now, Nyria. We cannot go back until you're twenty-six years old and when you give birth."

I jumped out of my seat and yelled, "*Birth?*"

"Yes, did you not hear that part of the story, or—"

"Yeah, but, oh my god . . . we made love twice now. Am I pregnant?"

"No, you cannot have children with me until you are twenty-six. That is the proper age for Newbians to come to impregnate their seeds. Remember, my elders sent me here two years early. You're only twenty-four, so we have another two years."

My heart was beating faster than a speeding bullet. When he said I have another two years it started to beat normally again.

"I need a drink, and not water."

He laughed and stopped me before I went into the kitchen to get something to drink.

"Nyria, I have to go. I hear my elders calling me. Something is wrong. I must leave right away."

Feeling his anxiety, I answered, "Oh, all right. They can send you messages in your mind too?"

"Yes, they can, just as all Newbians can. I'm glad we had an hour to ourselves today for me to explain everything. I have to go see what they want. I will be back later. I promise."

I knew he had to go. I could feel the anxiety running through him, so they must have been very concerned with something.

"OK, I will see you when you get back. I hope everything is OK. I love you."

That caught him off guard. This was the second time I told him I loved him.

"I love you too, with all my heart, Nyria."

He gave me a kiss and walked to the balcony doors to open his realm.

Right before he walked through, he blew me a kiss and I caught it.

Then he was gone.

I continued to the kitchen to grab a drink. I needed something. I had taken a lot in today.

As I was searching through my cupboards for some powdered juice, I stopped and praised myself.

"I'm getting the hang of this blocking thing. Yeah, me!"

I had to give myself credit. When we stared into each other's eyes, I felt in control. And I liked it.

Not finding any powdered juice, I decided to go to the corner store to buy some. Plus, I needed a walk after all that. I grabbed my keys and headed out of my apartment.

As I walked out of the building, I noticed his car sitting in the parking lot. I went over to it, just to admire my favourite sports car. I giggled to myself, and turned to walk down the street. I was on cloud nine. I was one of billions to experience this type of thing. Having a Newbian as a boyfriend was something out of the ordinary.

I opened the door to the little corner store and saw Lisa laughing with a man I had never met before.

"Hey, Lisa."

"Oh my gosh, Nyria, long time no see. Sorry I haven't called, but I've been busy. As you can see."

She nudged toward the man she had been laughing with.

"Ah. Gotcha."

I didn't want to step on her toes, so I waited for her to introduce us before I asked who he was.

"Hey honey, this is one of my best friends, Nyria, who I was telling you about. Nyria, this is Kevin Laung."

"Nice to meet you," I said as I held out my hand.

"The pleasure is all mine. I've heard a lot about you from Lisa."

"Oh really? Hope it was all good." I gave her a casual wink. "So, how did you guys meet?"

Before he answered, Lisa took my hand and led me outside the store. I didn't understand why it was a secret, but I followed anyway.

"Listen, you gonna be home later? I seriously need to talk to you."

"Yeah, I'll be home. Everything all right?" She was acting a little suspicious.

"Oh yeah, I'm fine, but it's a long story, and since you're my best friend, I think you should know how we met. Even though I'm not supposed to say anything, I don't care. You're my girl."

I was even more confused than before.

"OK, I'm just buying juice then I'm going home. What time will you be up?"

Peering around, she answered, "Actually, I'll walk up with you. If that's OK?"

"Sure, but what about him?"

She didn't answer me, she just took off into the store. I could see her mouth moving but I didn't know what she was saying to him.

They came out together.

"I'll see you later, honey." She gave him a kiss and he waved at me without saying a word. Lisa still had her lips planted on his. When she finally let the poor guy breathe, he smiled and said, "It was really nice to have met you, Nyria. See you later, Lisa."

"Nice to have met you too, Kevin."

She gave him one last wave as he drove off in his blue Honda Civic.

"Lisa, I need to get some juice. give me a second and I will be right out."

"Yep, sure."

I went back into the store to buy the juice. I exited the store to find her watching Kevin drive out of sight.

"So, what's new?"

She didn't answer until we got around the corner of the little store.

"You're not going to believe me, but you need to promise me something first."

"OK, I promise, whatever it is."

"You can't tell a soul what I'm about to tell you, Nyria. No one."

She was breathing heavy. I knew that whatever it was, it was top secret.

"I promise, Lisa. Just spit it out."

She swallowed a hard gulp, spit, and began.

"OK. Kevin . . ."

Another

"Well, how do I say this without sounding ridiculous. Umm . . . he's from a different planet."

She stopped to see my reaction. I didn't react at all, but I couldn't tell her why. I realized that if I didn't act like this story was weird to me, she might think I knew something about it.

As it was, she wasn't supposed to tell anyone and there she was telling me.

"Whatever," I said.

"I know. I know it sounds like I'm crazy, but it's true, Nyria. He even walked through the wall in my bedroom."

She so was eager to tell me she was walking circles around me.

"All right, Lisa, stop circling me, you're making me dizzy. You're right, it does sound crazy. He sounds like he suites you."

"Ha ha ha. Funny, Nyria. I'm serious."

"I know, Lisa, continue. What else did he say?"

She started to walk a little straighter, not circling me anymore.

"Well, he's here to take me back with him, but . . . I have to have a child first, 'cause they can't where he's from."

I interrupted her. I knew what she was talking about. I had to make it seem like I didn't.

"He wants to have a baby with you? And then he's taking you away? Whoa!"

I had to stop her from talking; people were coming out of the building.

"Just wait until we get into my apartment, OK?"

Two men exited the building, one grinning from ear to ear at us.

"Good day, ladies," one of the men said.

Lisa and I both replied at the same time. "Hello."

We hurried inside, and didn't say another word until we were in my apartment. She didn't even give me time to put the juice on the counter before she started again.

"Nyria, I'm already pregnant."

I dropped the juice on the floor. I didn't look at her. I just stared at the powder coming out of the bag.

"Nyria, did you hear me?"

"Yes, Lisa. When? How long have you been seeing him?"

"Well, you know me, right? One day I meet him at the club and, ah, he lingered at me. The next thing I knew we were in the club's bathroom stall getting it on. Weird too, because we came right off the floor. Like we were floating or something. Then I was exhausted and so was he. I must have asked him to come back to my place, 'cause the next morning I woke up in my own bed with him lying beside me. Oh yeah, I can't forget the feeling I had. I felt bodystoned. Like I was high or something."

I was half leaning onto the counter. She kept talking.

"And now I know what he's feeling. I can feel all his emotions. Oh, and I can't forget, we can send each other messages through our thoughts."

I didn't look at her until she called my name.

"Nyria?"

I turned to her with a sincere look on my face.

"Lisa, you know you're my best friend, right?"

"Well, I hope so. I'm not crazy, Nyria, it's all true!"

Holding my hands out, I reached for her.

"Wait, Lisa . . . I know. I know you're telling the truth. Oh my . . . did you tell anyone else?"

"No! You're the only one."

"You're sure?"

"Yes, I'm sure. I'd know if I told someone . . . *pffft*."

"Sorry, but I just had to make sure. You know you're not supposed to tell anyone about this, right?"

She looked at me as though I told her I already knew.

"What are you saying, Nyria? Did he . . . no, you just met him. How do you know I'm not supposed to tell anyone? And why aren't you more in shock at all this?"

I took a deep breath, knowing I might regret this, but she was going through the same thing as I was.

"OK, listen, I already know about this. He's from Newbia, and he's here to take you back with him because his realm can't bear children."

She crossed her arms and became a little bit defensive.

"How do you know this?"

"I know because I met someone from the same place who is also here to take me back to Newbia."

She turned around then back again to look straight into my eyes.

"You're not old enough. Kevin told me you have to be twenty-six years old before they come to get you."

She was right, but my story had a different edge.

"I know, you're absolutely right, Lisa, but the reason Sebastian is here . . . well, his elders told him to come. He lost connection with me six years ago and they thought something was wrong . . ."

"That's *you*? Kevin told me about you, but he didn't say a name."

"What do you mean he told you about me?"

Holding her chest and clearing her throat, she continued. "All's he said was that there's a legend of a young woman from

Earth and a young man from Newbia who lost their chemical connection, and that—"

She stopped in her own tracks.

"What? Lisa, what?"

I grabbed her arms, squeezing them with my hands and shaking her to spit it out.

"He comes to find her and she gets pregnant right away and . . . something bad happens and they kill the Newbian."

By this time I was now standing defensively, still holding her in my grip.

"*What?* I don't think Kevin got it right. I'm not pregnant and Sebastian is not going to be killed. He didn't do anything wrong. They told him to come here and he did, so you can tell Kevin . . ."

She now had me by the arms.

"Nyria, sorry, you're probably right. I'm so sorry, I'm not trying to upset you. I love you, girl."

My buzzer rang.

"You want me to get that, Nyria?"

"No, I'll get it."

I went to push it, and held it for a while. I slowly slumped down on my sofa, Lisa still standing by the kitchen entrance.

"Knock knock," from the other side of the door. Sebastian's voice.

Lisa opened the door, and there he stood. Before he could say a word, she greeted him.

"Hi, you must be . . . umm . . ."

Holding his hand out to greet her, he finished her sentence.

"Sebastian. Is Nyria in there?"

"Oh yeah, come on in."

She opened the door so he could fit his muscular body through, and looked him up and down as he walked by. I knew by the way she looked at him she was thinking *Yummy!*

"What's wrong, Nyria?" he asked, taking a stance beside me.

"Well, Sebastian, I'm not sure. Ha! This is Lisa Fry, my other best friend. She came over today and told me some scary shit."

He could feel my emotions going crazy. He couldn't figure which one to focus on because there were so many, more than usual. He glanced over at Lisa, who stood there staring at both of us.

"What did you say to her?" he demanded.

"Well, you know Kevin Laung, right?"

"Yes."

"Well, that's my boyfriend now. I was just telling her about him. I found out she already knew about Newbia. Oh, and I started to tell her about the legend he told me, and—"

"Wait." He stared into my eyes and said, "I don't know how far she got in telling you about the legend, but I have to tell you something."

I looked deep into his eyes, blocking him so we didn't put on a show in front of Lisa.

"What is it, Sebastian?"

He lowered his head and answered. "The elders needed to talk to me about you. I don't know how to say this, but . . . you're pregnant."

My expression was frozen. I stood in shock.

"What? How? I thought you said I cannot get pregnant because we both had to be twenty-six."

"Yes, I know I told you that. But I was wrong. They said it might have something to do with me losing connection with you six years ago. They're not 100 percent sure that's the real reason, but they do know that you're pregnant. They can see and feel all the emotions human seeds and Newbians have. The oldest of them all was feeling ill. She was seen by our medical doctor, Irene. She told her that whoever's feelings she was connecting with was pregnant and that something abnormal was taking place.

"My parents and all the elders had a meeting and asked me to connect with you, so I did. I stood in front of them all. They could feel and see the colours of our emotions together, and they felt another.

"The oldest elder came and stood by my side and placed her hand on my stomach. She was thrown across the room. We all went rushing to her aid when she told us that my seed, which is you, is pregnant. They were all shocked. This has never happened before.

"Ah . . ." I was lost for words. I couldn't speak. My mind went blank and my body went numb.

Lisa had her hand over her mouth. Before he said another word, Lisa came to my side.

"I should go, Nyria. You both have a lot to talk about. Give me a call later. It was nice to have met you Sebastian. Take care of her for me."

"Lisa, you don't have to leave."

"Yeah, well . . . Kevin is waiting for me. Plus, you guys need to be alone to talk about this."

I stood up and threw my arms around her waist, hugging her tighter and tighter.

"Don't tell anyone about all of this, Lisa. You know what I mean."

She stared into my eyes.

"I promise. But can't I tell Kevin?"

Sebastian interrupted.

"He already knows. Everyone knows. He will tell you the rest when you meet up with him. Thanks, Lisa. It was nice meeting you too."

He unwrapped my arms from around her and pressed me against him. Lisa headed for the door. Before she walked out, she turned to me.

"Everything will be OK, Nyria. Love you!"

She closed the door behind her.

Still standing in the middle of my living room with Sebastian's arms wrapped around me, I asked, "What now?"

He stared at my lips and answered. "The elders need to talk to you and they are coming here tonight."

Searching for his eyes so he knew to look at me, I grew confused.

"Why can't I go there instead? And why do they need to talk to me?"

"Because they've never had this happen before and they are concerned for you and the baby. After tapping into your emotions, which wasn't very easy for them to do, they saw a lot of interesting things. Many colours of which no one has ever seen. I was giving off a lot of emotions—Newbians usually gave off a few, but mine were the same as yours. This is all new to them. One even said the legend is coming true. What that means, I have no idea. I did ask, but got the cold shoulder. They are not coming here to hurt you, Nyria. I will never let anyone hurt you. Ever. Plus, they always come in a peaceful manner."

I had nothing to say. I was stiff as a board.

What next? I knew Sebastian could feel my emotions because I could feel his.

"Weird how your friend is a seed too, huh?"

I just looked at him and said nothing. He cracked a smile, but it disappeared when he saw my facial expression. I looked as though I was lost in space. His expression changed in an instant, and I knew he sensed something.

He scoured the room as if something were about to happen.

"Nyria, come sit down, please. They are here."

Mine Now!

Just as Sebastian sat down with me on the sofa, the wall became wavy. Two women and two men wearing white cloaks came through my living room wall.

I watched Sebastian's face as they entered. He seemed to not recognize them.

"Who are you?" Sebastian protested.

One of the women stepped forward and spoke. "Respect your elders, dear. Do not question who we are."

Sebastian held me tighter. Something wasn't right. I knew this because I could feel his anxiety. I sent a message to him but I don't think he got it.

The woman closest to us moved beside me and held her hand out.

"So, you are the one everyone's been feeling. What is your name, dear?"

My body was shaking as I spoke. "Nyria Crowell."

"Well, it's nice to have finally met you. We are the elders of Newbia."

She motioned at the three that stood closer to the wall. They didn't move a muscle. It was like they were statues.

Sebastian was staring at all of them. Something was a little off, but he couldn't put his finger on it. They looked just like the elders, but . . .

The woman reached out for me.

"I felt a baby brewing deep within you, my dear. You are twenty-four years old?"

"Yes. Is something wrong?"

"No, we just don't understand how this could have happened. This is all new to us, my dear, and we want to make sure the baby—and you, of course—are OK. Let's see you. Please stand up."

Sebastian held me tighter than before he shouted at her.

"Why do you want her to stand? She's fine where she is."

Again the woman spoke, a bit sharper this time.

"How dare you question my authority. I am not talking to you, and this will be your last warning."

Sebastian wasn't buying it. The elders would never speak so rudely, even if he was out of line. He stood up, strong as an ox, and stared into the woman's eyes.

The man standing to the right of him grabbed his arm and pulled him forward. The man standing to his left grabbed his other arm and held him in protest.

Sebastian was now fighting to get out of their grip. I jumped to my feet to help, but the woman took hold of me, saying, "You will never see him again, and that disgusting baby will never see the light of day."

I tried to free myself but, she was overpowering me. The other woman opened the wall behind her.

"No!"

Sebastian was fighting harder than before, telling them to let me go. His feet were lifted in the air by the two men holding him.

The woman swiftly grabbed me. With me firmly in her grip, we went through the wavy wall.

I was gone.

"*Nyria!*" Sebastian yelled at the top of his lungs. He gathered all his might and swung the men to the ground. He landed on his feet and dashed for the wall, but the second woman was in his way.

He rammed right through her.

The wall was back to normal. He left a huge hole in it. When he realized he couldn't go through to where they took me, he went mad. He jumped on top of the man closest to him and snapped his neck.

Meanwhile, the woman was helping the other man get his feet, trying to escape. Sebastian grabbed the two of them by their heads and slammed them together, knocking the woman unconscious.

He punched the man in the throat, damaging his air passage, which left him dead.

He grabbed the woman and opened the wall to his realm. He was heading home with the stranger flung over his shoulder to get the help from his elders. He took the woman for information.

Home!

"Help, please! Someone help!" Sebastian screamed at the top of his lungs as he entered the centre of town.

The elders were getting ready to leave. They were coming to meet us at my apartment, not realizing I had just been kidnapped. The oldest elder, Cameron, ran to his side as he plopped the unknown woman down on the ground.

"They took her!"

"Who took her?"

Cameron demanded to know what he was yelling about.

"Them."

He pointed to the unconscious woman. Cameron unmasked her to find a Lubrian in disguise. Her face had big black eyes and a small round mouth.

"Oh my. Let's get out of the audience."

Cameron motioned to the guard behind him to pick the woman up and take her to the town hall. There were too many people standing around that didn't need to see this.

As they entered the hall, the other Newbian elders met up with them. There were four elders on the throne. The oldest was Cameron, then Luc, Jules and Amy, all in their late hundreds.

"What is happening here, my fellow brother?" Luc questioned.

"These Lubrians took Nyria. Please, help me!" Sebastian cried.

"Oh no! They found out about the baby, didn't they?" Jules uttered.

Cameron ordered the guard to place the woman in a room. "We will interrogate her. Wake her up!" he demanded as he slapped the Lubrian across the face.

Cameron went to Sebastian and placed a hand on his shoulder.

"Please let us do our job here. We will find her, but you need to get your strength up in order to fight for her. They will kill her, my boy. They know she is carrying a child . . ."

Sebastian interrupted, asking, "Why did they take her? What is she to them?"

Amy took Sebastian's arm and awaited Cameron's approval.

"Let me explain to him, please, my brother."

Cameron nodded as the others entered the room holding the Lubrian.

"What is going on? We need to go after the Lubrians now!" Sebastian felt there was no need of a story while I was in the Lubrian's guard.

"Wait, Sebastian, you need to know why they took her. She is the . . ."

She sighed. It was difficult to say.

"What?"

"She is the legend of which we never told anyone about."

His eyes grew wide with anticipation and concern. The legend!

"What is the legend? No one would ever speak of it, so tell me . . . please."

Amy cleared her throat quickly, as she could tell Sebastian was growing impatient.

"The legend states that a woman from Earth will come to Newbia bearing a child within her. Something we've always been waiting for. She has the power to save our realm. Sebastian . . . Nyria is our greatest creation. Our queen!"

He froze as the word *queen* fell off Amy's lips.

"What?"

She smiled at him, her eyes filled with joy.

"We know how important she is to you . . . and to us. This is why we were coming to see her. We wanted to speak to both of you, to tell you this. But unfortunately the Lubrians found out somehow and they don't want us to have her. They know we will overpower them with her on our side. And you, Sebastian, that makes you our king. You need to stay here while we find Nyria. You cannot be in harm's way."

"I don't care what I am. All I know is that she is my love of my life and she's carrying my child. They have her and I will not sit back and do nothing. I will fight to the death for her. You cannot stop me, either."

Placing her hand on his shoulder, she whispered, "And we won't, but getting upset with us will not help. You need to go to your parent's house and wait there until—"

"I'm not going anywhere. I want to hear what this thing has to say. They have the most precious thing to me—Nyria. So, I am not going to— *Ouch!*"

"What's wrong, Sebastian?" she asked as he buckled over in pain.

"They are hurting her. I can feel it. *Ouch!*"

Rushing to his side, she helped him to his feet.

"Hurry, come with me."

She brought him to where the other elders were interrogating the Lubrian. He hurried alongside her as they entered a bright room with wires everywhere.

The Lubrian was hissing at them. She was tied to a bed completely naked, exposed as what she really was: a skinny, fragile skeleton, grey from head to toe. Her big black eyes searched for a way out. Her small lips curled as she hissed at them.

"Ugh! She's one ugly Lubrian," Sebastian stated.

"They all look like this," Cameron said. He was standing over her with a cup of water, threatening to pour it on her if she didn't tell them where they took Nyria.

Lubrians could not touch water or their skin would burn to the bone.

"I will tell you nothing, you fucking insect," the Lubrian hissed.

"Give me the water, I will drown her in it!" Sebastian yelled as he leaped toward Cameron.

"No, my boy! Who let him in here, anyway?"

"I did, brother . . . I need you to see this," Amy said, pointing to Sebastian.

Sebastian's knees grew weak and he let out an awful howl.

Cameron requested an answer. "What is this?"

Amy didn't hesitate. "He is feeling Nyria's pain. The Lubrians are hurting her in some way. He's the key in finding her, my brother."

"You'll never find her, you fucking insect," the Lubrian hissed again.

Sebastian gathered strength behind his fist and punched the Lubrian in the face.

Luc grabbed his arm and shouted, "Sebastian! My boy, please let us be the one to hurt this creature. I don't want blood on your hands."

"I don't care, I'll kill this . . . this foul thing."

He grabbed a wire that was attached to its head and yanked it as hard as he could, pulling a long piece of skin off the fragile skeleton. It screamed and twitched from the pain.

"Remove him from here!" Cameron called to the guards.

Sebastian was ready for them, balling his hands into fists.

Jules came to his rescue.

"I will take him out. Let me calm him down. There is no need for us to fight, Sebastian. We know what we're doing. Please, my boy, come with me."

His hands were now relaxed. He agreed to go with her. But before he left the room he said, "If it doesn't talk, I will make it. I want Nyria back and I will do anything I can. I'm sorry to fight against you, but she is my everything."

He looked at the Lubrian one more time and declared, "I'm going to kill you and your kind, I promise."

He turned to Jules and they exited the room side by side.

"Please, Sebastian, let us do what we can. I know you love her and she loves you. She needs you to calm down before you hurt someone, even yourself. We will find her, I promise. She will be in your arms again. I just need you to stay out of that room until we have the answers we need. If for any reason the Lubrian will not cooperate, I give you my word: you can do as you wish upon it. But until then, promise you will listen to me."

He hesitated for a second but nodded in agreement.

"Thank you, my boy. Now go home to your parents and tell them what is happening. We will gather all the warriors together, to get our queen back safe and sound. One more thing, ask your mother Charlene to go to the medicine doctor, Irene. Tell her I asked for her to cast a spell on Nyria's friends so they don't notice her missing. All we need is for them to worry about her too. I know they would start a search, which will cause more problems than need be. Go!"

He grabbed her hand and gently whispered, "I can't take this, the pain they are inflicting on her. I feel so weak."

Grabbing his hand, she whispered in his ear, "Be strong, Sebastian. I believe you can. Now go!"

He let her hand go and bolted out of the town hall. He ran as fast as he could to his parents' house, where he would tell them everything Jules asked of him.

His mother called Irene and relayed the message.

Sebastian fell to his knees. The pain was too much. He collapsed in the hallway to his old bedroom.

His parents ran to his aid. They carried him to his bed, where he lay there lifeless, just as Nyria was in Lubria.

Sorry

An alarm rang. Sebastian jumped up from his bed. Surveying his old room, he wondered how he had made it to his bed. The pain was now gone. All that was running through his mind was me. Sitting at the end of his bed, he tried sending me a message.

Nyria, I'm coming to get you, baby. Please let me know if you're OK. I'm so sorry I let them take you. I will do whatever it is to have you in my arms again. Nyria, I love you.

After sending the telepathic message, he wobbled out to the living room, where he found a note on the coffee table.

Sebastian,

Everyone is at the town square. Your father and I didn't want to wake you. When you read this, meet us there.

Love, Mom xoxo

He hurried out the front door. Heading toward the town square, he could hear people gathering. As he approached, he noticed an army of warriors getting ready to board a ship that looked like a spherical 757 Boeing.

Startling him, a little girl pulled at his pant leg, shouting, "They are going to get our queen. I can't wait to meet her. I heard she's beautiful and she's having a baby."

He smiled at her as he hustled toward the elders and his parents.

"Oh, Sebastian, they know where she is. The Lubrian told them before they killed it," his mother cried.

He grabbed her in his arms and kissed her forehead.

"I'm going with them."

Letting her quickly leave, he headed toward Cameron.

"I'm going with them, and I won't take no for an answer."

Cameron stood in front of him in protest.

"My boy, you cannot go, you have never been trained to fight. We cannot lose you. Especially now."

He stared into Sebastian's eyes, feeling his emotions. He knew what he was planning. Cameron took it upon himself to grab the attention of three guards. He motioned for them to grab Sebastian. He knew he'd try to get on the ship, even if he had to fight.

The three guards rushed over, gripping Sebastian as tight as they could.

Sebastian fought his hardest, but the struggle wasn't enough. He yelled at them to let him go, but the ship was taking off.

As the ship flew above, the guards released him.

He fell to his knees and cried—the most hurtful cry a man could make.

"Please bring her back unharmed," he yelled as the warriors gave a salute.

The warriors waved from the opening at the back of the ship: a salute goodbye.

Sebastian pushed his way through the crowd to be by himself. He leaned up against the town hall, pondering what to do next. He raised his hand to the wall to open the portal to Earth and walked through.

His mother called out to him, but he was gone.

"Where did he go?" she asked her husband.

"I don't know, dear, but he's pretty upset. I hope he doesn't do anything stupid."

My Apartment

He didn't have to knock, no one was home. My apartment was empty. He could feel me everywhere.

Entering my room he lay on the bed, squeezing my pillow to get my scent. Crying rapidly, he eventually fell into a deep sleep.

Something woke him up about an hour later. A message.

Sebastian, I love you. If I die, please don't ever forget me. I love you more than ever. I'm so happy you came into my life, even if it was only a few days. I felt you there, always. Now that I know who you are, you're the best thing that's ever happened to me.

I was dying.

But something seemed wrong.

Sensing something, he jumped out of bed. Someone was there.

There was a dirty plate and glass left on my end table. He hadn't noticed it when he first went into my room.

I didn't do that, he thought to himself.

Who is here?

He began to investigate, looking around the house.

The apartment door opened Sebastian hid behind the door, ready to slug the person entering.

The young man was whistling to himself. The door began to close behind him, and Sebastian took a quick look to make sure it wasn't someone he knew.

He punched the intruder in the back of the head, and he fell with a thud. He leaned over him and recognized his face. It was another Newbian.

"Adam? What is he doing here? How does he know Nyria?" he asked out loud, a bit stunned. At this point, no one was to be trusted.

He tied Adam to a kitchen chair, and slapped him in the face to wake him up.

Adam came to, and found Sebastian sitting in front of him on another chair with a knife in his hand. Surprised, Adam began blurting out information.

"I'm so sorry, man. I didn't think they were going to hurt her. I swear!"

Sebastian was surprised.

"What . . . you mean you're responsible for Nyria being taken?"

"I thought they were just gonna take the baby. They told me that's all they wanted. She was supposed to be my seed, not yours. I swear, if I'd known they were going to hurt her, I wouldn't have told them anything."

Sebastian gripped the knife so hard his knuckles cracked. The sound would have gone up one side of you and down the other.

"Of course . . . you knew about the baby. Every Newbian knows. You betrayed us to them, those fucking Lubrians?"

He roared and jabbed the knife into Adam's knee.

"AHHH!"

Sebastian didn't care if anyone heard him. Adam was going to die.

"Please man, please don't kill me. I didn't know, I swear."

"Shut up, you fucking traitor. If Nyria was supposed to be your seed, you wouldn't have told them anything. She could die because of you. You'll pay if she does, I can promise you that."

Hearing the word *die*, Adam screamed, "Help! Someone help!"

Sebastian nailed him square in his jaw and Adam's four front teeth went flying.

"That'll shut you up for a while."

Chuckling, he leaped up from his chair and grabbed a hand towel to cover Adam's mouth so no one would hear him screaming. Especially as it was time to die.

Adam was bleeding all over the kitchen floor, crying like a baby. Sebastian taunted him as he paced back and forth.

"Wanna cry a little harder? I don't believe you, Adam."

He stabbed his other knee. Adam let out a long cry under the hand towel.

Leaning toward Adam's face, Sebastian whispered, "The next one is gonna be the one that kills you, you fucking waste of breath."

Hate began to reign over Sebastian's emotions. Thoughts of me clouded his head. He wanted to go home to find out if they had found me or not, but he couldn't leave Adam there alive.

He took one last look at Adam's face. Tears filled Adam's eyes, as they both knew what was coming.

"I don't care if they kill me when I return to Newbia. As long as you die!"

Sebastian raised his hand, the knife held sideways, and sliced Adam's throat. He let him bleed out.

Washing his hands after his brutal kill, he watched Adam choke to death, then laid his hand on the wall to return to his realm.

He arrived in the town square. The streets were empty, just like his heart. He didn't care that Adam's dead body was laying in my apartment. He was so cold-hearted at this point that he had no more care left for anyone but me.

Racing into the town hall he found the elders standing there with disappointment on their faces. They knew what he had done.

Jules was the first to talk.

"We are very disappointed with you, Sebastian. We know you're going through a lot right now. but killing your own doesn't solve anything. You know what must happen now, don't you?"

He didn't answer. Turning to Cameron, he asked, "Have they found her yet?"

Cameron walked to Sebastian and held his hands out to him.

"My boy, why have you done this? We know what he did. It wasn't your choice to take his life. I'm sorry to say this, but . . ."

He paused. It hurt him to say the words. Cameron knew deep down he would have done the same.

Distancing himself from Sebastian, he commanded the guards to take him into custody.

Sebastian didn't have any more fight in him. He went peacefully.

"It doesn't matter anyway. They have her!" he yelled as they dragged him out of the room.

Loud noises shot through the skies. The warriors were returning. In a matter of seconds, people filled the town square.

Sebastian's eyes grew wide. He broke loose of the guards and ran out of the hall.

The warriors held their weapons high as they preached, "She is home! Our queen is home!"

Sebastian ran to see her.

"Nyria! You found her?" he asked one of the warriors exiting the ship.

"Yes, we found her."

Sebastian's heart was racing, waiting to see my face.

The warriors were coming off the ship two by two. He saw my fragile body lying in the arms of the head warrior.

Sebastian ran up to him and swept me out of his hands, looking down at my face. I was pale and broken. My eyes were closed. The only movement was my chest moving up and down as I breathed.

The medical doctor, Irene, came running to my aid.

"Put her down, Sebastian, I need to take her to the hospital!"

As they lay my motionless body on the ambulance stretcher, I began to open my eyes. Sebastian made sure he was the first person I saw.

"Hi baby."

My eyes rolled back as I slipped into a deep sleep. Sighing out of disbelief and frustration, he kissed my lips.

Irene interrupted him by laying her hand on his back.

"We need to take her now, Sebastian, please."

Moving out of the way, the guards rushed to his side and swooped me out of his hands. Glancing back toward the elders, he hoped for redemption. They turned their backs on him and lowered their heads in shame.

One guard politely said, "Sorry, but you have to come with us now."

Tears were running down his face. He felt no regret for what he did, just happiness.

I was going to be OK.

Before the guards escorted him away, he yelled to the elders.

"How did you find her?"

No answers followed. The guards had hold of his arms, tugging him away.

"I'm going, geez, can't wait to kill me, huh? You bunch of killers. He deserved to die and you know it."

I was now in the ambulance being attended to. I heard him yelling. I came to like a shock wave went through my body. I held my hand out to Irene and leaned toward her so she could hear what I wanted to say.

"Sebastian . . . I want Sebastian."

Irene had no choice but to do as I wished. She knew who and what I meant to her people.

Jumping out of the ambulance, Irene began to wail. "Stop! Our queen has spoken."

Everyone came to a standstill to listen.

"She wants Sebastian."

Cameron came forward in protest and was about to say something when Luc took his arm.

"My brother, she wants him. She is our queen. We must do as she says. We cannot kill him for loving her. Even though he went against our rules. I'm sure she would want her king by her side."

Luc waited for Cameron to respond. Everyone waited for him to say something. Silence blew through the crowd, all eyes on him.

Sebastian was even staring at him, waiting.

"Let it be known: the queen is finally here to rule over all of Newbia. She asks for her King Sebastian, and . . ."

He paused and looked straight at Sebastian.

"Sebastian she shall have. Set him free!"

Everyone who was standing in the town square let out a roar of cheers as he ran to the ambulance to meet me, his beloved, loving queen. *Me!*

He approached me and carefully took my hand in his.

"I am here, Nyria."

I slowly opened my eyes to see his face glowing like the night moon. Smiling at him, I gave a light squeeze to his warm hands.

"Sebastian?"

That's all I said before my ECG scanner flatlined.

"Nyria? *Nyria? NOOOOO!*"

Day 1

His heart felt heavy as he watched me slip away. He stared at my lifeless body. Irene leaped into the ambulance, almost knocking him over.

"*Move!* I need to work on her."

Sebastian stood frozen in time. He was in shock; he didn't know what to do or say. My heart wasn't beating anymore. My chest wasn't pulsating up and down. I was gone.

Irene yelled to the ambulance driver to speed off toward the hospital.

"We need to step on it!" Irene demanded.

The back door swung closed as Irene continued to work. Lights were flashing and the siren sounded as they pulled away.

Sebastian stood with his eyes glued to the ambulance doors. His mother Charlene came running to him and wrapped him in her arms.

"Sebastian, honey, come with me. They will do their best, sweetie, I'm sure. We'll follow behind them. Come on!"

Sluggishly, he sat in the passenger seat of her car, paralyzed by the situation. Charlene turned the ignition over and flew down the streets full throttle toward the hospital.

The car ride was quiet. The only noise was the tires squealing as she cut corners without pressing the brakes.

Arriving at the hospital, Sebastian jumped out of the car and threw open the hospital doors.

A nurse approached him with good news.

"Nyria's heart began to pulsate as soon as she arrived. You can see her after Irene comes out."

Sebastian seemed lost in thought. He heard the tiny nurse, but there was no response. He collapsed in the nearest chair.

Charlene was immediately at his side.

"What did they say, honey?"

He mumbled his words together, managing to say, "They said her heart was beating again."

Charlene grinned from ear to ear and clapped her hands together.

"See, baby, she'll be fine. I just knew she'd pull through."

Still slouched over in the chair, he said, "Huh!"

That's all he said before thinking of ways to kill the Lubrians.

Hours passed.

Nurses were running from one room to the next like chickens with their heads cut off. Finally Irene made an appearance.

"Sebastian?"

He stood when she said his name.

"Nyria is in stable condition now, that's the good news. The bad news is she is in a coma, and the baby . . . well . . . they have it. They took the embryo from her."

His face went pale.

"They took the baby?"

"Yes, but she needs all the support she can get. If you come with me I can let you see her, but only for a short time."

Taking a deep breath, he waved at Irene to lead the way.

Walking into my hospital room, his chest became restricted and chills ran through his body. His eyes were full of tears, as he tried to fight back the anger. Finding his place beside my bed, he placed his hands over my stomach and whispered, "I promise,

Nyria, I will get our baby back. And those Lubrians will pay for everything. I love you. Pull through this and come back to me."

Wiping his face of the tears running down his cheeks, he glanced up at Irene and asked if I could hear him.

"Yes, she can hear you. But it's time to leave. You can come back later."

He leaned forward to kiss me on my dried, cracked lips and to tell me he loved me—always and forever.

Slowly, he left the room. He stood by my door for a moment, then headed for the front doors. Charlene watched him walk by without a word.

Trailing behind him, she found him standing just outside the hospital doors.

"What is it, son?"

"I need you to stay here until I come back. I will call you whenever I get a chance. There's something I must do. Will you do that for me?"

"Yes, of course, but what is it that you need to do? Nyria needs you to—"

There was no time for a dispute.

"Mom, trust me, please. I have to go. I will call you later. Oh, and I need your car."

He held his hands out for the keys. She hesitated to pass them over; his demeanour was sketchy. But she eventually gave in.

"Thanks, Mom."

As the keys touched the palm of his hand, he jogged toward the parked car and took off, squealing the tires.

Charlene held her hand over her mouth, wondering if she had done the right thing.

He drove to an older style building about a mile away from the hospital. Rushing out of the car and up the stairs, he opened the doors to find men of all ages training for battle.

Silence fell over the room but for whispers travelling around the warriors.

An older man in his mid-hundreds walked over to him.

"May I help you?"

"Yes, I want you to teach me the ropes on killing Lubrians," Sebastian blurted out.

The man stepped back, now realizing who Sebastian was.

He bowed his head and said, "Of course. When do you want to start?"

"Right now."

The man was shocked as his confidence.

"Oh. Well, class is over in five minutes, do you want to come back tomorrow?"

Sebastian was determined to get started right away, so tomorrow was not an option.

"How about you have some of your guys stay behind to teach me. Class can end later. I want to start learning now."

The man nodded his head and turned to the warriors.

"Class, this is Sebastian. He will be training with us and class is not dismissed as of yet. Who will be the first to demonstrate?"

A heavyset warrior appeared from behind the crowd.

"I will."

He was Tyberrius, the head warrior of Newbia. He knew all there was to know about fighting and would be the best to train with Sebastian.

"Good then, let's go to the centre mat. Please remove your shoes and let's get started."

Before Sebastian's training began, the man announced, "In here you are no longer Sebastian. You are a warrior of Newbia. Do you understand that?"

"Yes."

"Good. My name is Issac Wiltz. I am the coach here. Whatever I say goes. You got that?"

"Yes."

"OK. Begin."

Sebastian and Tyberrius approached the middle of the mat. All the other warriors moved to stand against the walls.

Tyberrius was standing at full guard. Issac gave the orders.

"I want to see what you've got first. *Fight!*"

Day 2

Sore and exhausted, Sebastian thanked Issac and Tyberrius for their session.

He had learned a lot in two hours but, there was more training to be had. Bouncing into his mother's car, he headed to the hospital.

Reaching the hospital parking lot, he saw his mother leaving. With his face in a bunch, he quickly pulled into a space.

He bolted through the parked cars and approached her, gasping for air.

"Has anything changed, Mom?"

"No, Sebastian, she is still in a coma. The doctors were in and out of the room talking amongst themselves. They told me to go home to get some sleep. Your father is on his way here to pick me up. Where did you go?"

He didn't want to tell her, but he knew she'd soon find out.

"I went to see Issac and Tyberrius for some combat training."

Crossing her arms in disproval, she announced, "What for? You're not thinking of fighting? Are you?"

Just then his father, Bruce, pulled up.

"Not now, Mom. I will talk to you later, OK?"

Bruce knew something was up. He didn't say anything to either of them. He would wait to see if someone would be so kind as to fill him in. He rolled down his window and stuck his head out.

"How is she?"

"She's the same, Dad. I'm coming home with you guys. I will meet you there," Sebastian yelled before he dashed off.

They arrived at the house within seconds of each other. As Sebastian stepped out of the car, Bruce told his wife to go into the house.

"Sebastian, I want to talk with you."

"Dad, I'm tired."

"This will only take a minute. Please."

"What is it?"

"I know what you're going through, son, I just want you to promise me you won't do anything foolish."

Squinting his eyes, he took a deep breath before he commented on his father's words.

"You have no idea what I'm going through, Dad. Oh, and I won't do anything stupid. But if you think I'm going to sit back while they have my child and do nothing, you have another thing coming."

Bruce didn't want to upset him more then he already was, so he cracked a smile and said, "Whatever is on your mind, remember, I will always be here for you no matter what. You're my only son. If it's a war you're fighting, you don't have to do it alone."

He put his hand on Sebastian's shoulder and nudged him toward the house.

The shower was already running upstairs. His mother had turned it on for him, knowing he would want to clean up.

"Sebastian? Are you hungry?"

"No, Mom, I'm just going to take a shower then I'm going back to the hospital."

"You need to get some sleep, dear," she called out in a soft tone as she came rushing out of the kitchen.

"I will sleep at the hospital, Mom. Don't worry about me. I want to be with Nyria."

Bruce interrupted Charlene.

"Charlene! He's a grown boy. Let him go. He knows when he needs sleep."

His mother turned without replying and headed back into the kitchen.

"Go take a shower and I will see you tomorrow after work. And son? We love you."

"I love you too, Dad."

Sebastian headed up the stairs, threw his clothes off and stepped into the shower. He quickly cleaned up. When he was done, he stared into the mirror thinking of me, the Lubrians, and what they were doing to our child.

They had better not hurt our baby, he thought to himself as he searched the bathroom, trying to find a new toothbrush. He found one and quickly brushed up. Bolting down the stairs and grabbing his mother's car keys, he yelled out to his parents, "Goodnight, I will see you both later."

He leaped into his mother's car and drove ninety miles per hour toward the hospital.

Upon his arrival, he met Irene standing in front of my hospital door.

"How is she, Doc?"

"Nothing has changed. Are you staying with her tonight?"

"Yes, why?"

"I will have one of the orderlies bring up a cot for you to sleep on."

"That's OK, the chair will do," he replied. He opened my door and closed it quietly behind him.

Pulling a chair to the side of my bed, he gently held my hand and whispered close to my ear, "Nyria, baby, I'm here. Please open your eyes."

I didn't move an inch except for my stomach, up and down as I breathed.

He lay his head next to mine and watched me breathing. Soon, he fell fast asleep.

The Dream

In his deep sleep, he noticed a figure in the distance, walking toward him with hands stretched out.

Who was it?

"Nyria?" he called out.

As I got closer to him he could see that I was unbruised, glowing like the sun breaking through the sky clouds.

"Is this a dream?"

"Yes, Sebastian, but I am here."

The colours of emotions rained over us like a rainbow after a storm.

He held me close to him, asking, "How are you in my dream?"

"That doesn't matter right now. Sebastian, I need to tell you what happened. They have our child."

"I know. I will get our baby back, I promise."

"I knew you'd say that. That's why I am here. You need to know what I saw while they took me. Please have a seat."

A bench moved toward us, appearing at my wishes.

Sitting side by side, staring into each other's eyes, he had to know one thing first.

"Nyria, will you be in a coma forever?"

"I didn't know I was in a coma. Hmmm. That explains way I can hear everything around me but no one seems to hear me talking."

His face began to lower as guilt set in for not protecting me like he said he would. I could feel the agony behind his heart.

"Please don't beat yourself up. It's not your fault, Sebastian. They knew about me because of Adam."

"Adam!" He smirked at the name.

"Yeah, well, Adam won't be bothering you anymore."

"Why, what did you do?"

"It doesn't matter. He just won't be bothering us ever again. Wasn't he the guy you were telling me about? Who came into your work and got upset when I sent you those flowers?"

"Yes, he's the same guy. When they took me from my apartment to their realm, he was standing there with them, shaking their hands. I knew right away he had something to do with them kidnapping me."

"I know. He told on himself when I went back to your apartment. He showed up not realizing I was there."

"And?"

"And nothing. Tell me what you saw."

Through My Eyes

"After Adam left, they dragged me through their streets. It was very dark and muggy. It smelled very bad, like rotten garbage. It was very loud, too. People were everywhere. They were all talking but, there were too many voices.

"I could make out the woman who grabbed me and a man's voice. It was deeper than all the rest. Plus, he stayed with her the whole time. She called him Luther. I think he was her leader, because whatever he asked she did. I did hear at one point him call her Carmella, but, I only heard her name used once."

Just then they heard a voice.

"Sebastian? Sebastian? Wake up!"

The dream was over. He didn't even have a chance to say goodbye. He was calm and collected, but angry at the same time.

He was communicating with me while he slept. That seemed to be the closest thing he had to me right now. Nevertheless, someone had woken him up for a reason.

It better be a good one, he thought.

"What is it?"

His eyes were still unfocused. Things were still a blur.

"Honey, it's Mom."

"Mom?" Still disorientated, he mumbled, "I could talk to her . . . Nyria. She was in my dream. She was telling me about Lubria and her kidnappers. Why did you wake me? That could have been vital information. I don't even know if I will be able to talk to her again."

"Sorry dear, but Issac called this morning looking for you. He wants you to meet him. He said there's more to be done. The sooner the better. I'm sorry, dear."

Feeling bad for hissing at her, he grabbed her hand in apology.

"That's OK, Mom, I'm sorry. Are you staying here with Nyria?"

"Yes, go meet Issac. I will be here waiting for you to return. Did you sleep long?"

"I don't know."

He stood up to let his mother sit down.

"I will see you when I come back. Love you, Mom, and thanks."

"I love you too, son."

He leaned forward and gave her a kiss on the cheek. He kissed my lips and smoothed the hair from my face, uttering, "I love you, Nyria."

He left the room.

Sebastian trained for about six hours. Issac was pleased with his progress.

"Wow, my boy, you have a lot of talent for fighting. But you said you had never fought before."

"That's right, I haven't."

"Well, the more you practise the better you'll be. Tyberrius was surprised today when you used the water pistols as well as you did."

"Yeah, I thought the same thing. Tell me something, Coach. Does water really kill them?"

"Yes, water is their weakness. They don't have any on their planet, either. They are terrified of it. That's how we won the last war. We have enough water here to kill their entire world but we only choose to kill those who pose a threat to us. Not all of them are the same. Some of them would love to come live here. Their elders would never allow that to happen. If we kill their elders, well, no more war. It's hard to get to them, though. There's only two left, I believe. One of them is called Luther."

That name hit a chord in Sebastian's spine.

"Luther? He is one of their elders?"

"Yes, the other is one Carmella. Only, the story goes that she died from some type of plague years ago."

She's not dead, he thought to himself. He didn't mention anything to Issac, and wouldn't until he talked to me again, to find out if the woman's name was Carmella. He had to be sure before he gave information to anyone.

"All right, Coach, I will see you tomorrow. When do you think I'll be ready? I have to hurry; I feel like there's not much time. My child is in their custody and I don't trust what they'll do to it."

"Well, it all lies with you, Sebastian. You have to *feel* you are ready. Don't just say it, but believe you are. The warriors will fight with you. I hope you don't think you're doing this all on your own."

"No. The more help the better. I think I'm ready, but not a full 100 percent. I want to learn all I can, so when we attack I can kill those Lubrians and get my child back. I just need to hurry with training. For now, I will be with Nyria at the hospital if you need me for anything."

He smiled and presented his hand to shake.

"I see. I hope she comes out of this soon. And that the baby is OK."

Meeting his hand halfway, he thanked his coach and gave a wide smile back.

"Me too, thanks. See you tomorrow. Same time?"

"Same time."

Sebastian strolled to this mother's car and threw his belongs in the back seat. Deciding not to go home to shower, he drove to the hospital. He needed to talk to me again.

Heaviness weighed on his eyes. Training had taken a lot out of him today. Plus, he didn't get much sleep the night before.

Dodging past the nurses' station, he strolled to my room and opened the doors to find his mother sitting with me.

"Thanks, Mom, you can go home now. Get some rest, I'll call you later."

Waving her hand in front of her face, she giggled and said, "You smell bad, Sebastian. Go home and get cleaned up. I will wait here until you come back."

"Thanks, Mom, but I'll go home later. Oh, and if you come back before I go home, please bring me something to eat."

"I'll make one of your favourites: shepherd's pie."

She ran her fingers through his hair and quietly left the room. He sat in the chair next to me, whispering, "I'm here, baby." He wiped my forehead with his sweaty hands and laid his head down next to mine.

He was now back in the dream.

The Dream

I was sitting in the same place as before, waiting for him to return.

"Hello, my gorgeous Newbian hunk."

"Who?"

"You, silly!"

"Hi, beautiful." He blushed as he said it.

"Listen, I need you to focus, OK? I talked to my coach today and he said that one of the Lubrian elders was called Carmella. Was that the same name you told me before?"

"Yes, that's what Luther called her. Who's your coach and why do you have one?"

"I told you, I'm going to get our baby back and I need to know everything I can to win this war."

"I see. Well, if you want to win you need to know what I saw."

I took a deep breath, then began.

"OK, you know about Luther and Carmella, but what I need you to remember is that there are a lot of people around. The building they dragged me to had broken windows with lots of beat-up cars around it. They looked like cars from Earth. I know this because some had licence plates that read 'Nova Scotia's Playground' on them. It was the tallest building in their smelly city. You can't miss it, it towered over everything else. There were two men standing in front of it and about a dozen on the other side. I was taken through a long hall as we entered from the front. I saw a lot of wires hanging from the ceiling and a long tube coming toward me. I felt them go through my belly button. I knew they were taking my baby, but something was holding me down. I think I was frozen but I didn't feel them give me anything. The tube was in Carmella's hands when everything went blurry. After that, well, I saw you standing over me. I remember saying your name then things went dark. It was like I was in a nightmare. Something opened up, because I saw a bright light and Newbians. They were telling me to go back, that I wasn't supposed to be there. I turned around and saw you walking toward me. And here we are, talking in this dream."

Sebastian sighed.

"That was very helpful. Do you remember anything else?"

I held out my hand and told him he had to go.

"Something is happening to the baby, Sebastian, I can feel it."

He woke up ready for anything.

He kissed me on the forehead, then ran out the hospital doors, jumped into the car and bailed down the empty streets.

Finally, the car came to a rolling stop.

Lunging out, he forgot to turn off the engine. But it didn't matter; he needed to gather anyone willing to go to Lubria, and fast.

Ready

As the car came to a rolling stop, he saw Issac and Tyberrius standing with a few guards, laughing and talking. They could see the anxiety all over Sebastian's body and face as he lunged from the car.

"What's going on, Sebastian?" Issac demanded.

"We need to gather all the warriors, now. We have to go to Lubria to bring my child back. Right now."

Holding his hands out straight in front of him Issac protested, "Whoa, Sebastian."

"No, listen to me, I . . . I've been in communicating with Nyria. She just told me something is wrong. The baby is in trouble. We need to go now."

Everyone grew still as they waited for Issac's command.

"We leave in thirty minutes, men. Tyberrius, gather all the warriors and meet me at the town square. Go."

Tyberrius moved stealthily out of sight, gathering all the men willing to fight.

"Thanks, Coach. I will go to Earth to bring back all the Newbians willing to fight for their queen. I will meet you in thirty minutes," Sebastian added before stretching his hand toward the building and opening the realm to Earth. He ran through and ended up in my apartment.

Why did I come here? he asked himself.

A knock came to the door.

"Nyria! Nyria, it's Scott. You in there?"

"Oh shit."

Sebastian's eyes grew wide.

The smell in my apartment was lingering. Adam's corpse was beginning to rot.

Sebastian heard Scott on the other side of the door again.

"If you don't open this door, Nyria, I will break it down."

He was reacting aggressively due to the stench seeping from underneath my door.

Scott broke the door down and found Sebastian untying Adam's body from the chair.

"What the fuck?" Scott said.

"It's not what you think, Scott. I was—"

Sebastian was caught off guard as Scott came bulldozing toward him, but Sebastian was a lot stronger, Scott being merely human.

"Please listen to me, Scott."

Scott knew Sebastian was more than he could handle. It would take much more than his measly strength to break him.

"Where is Nyria? *Where is she?*"

Sebastian hesitated for a second, contemplating whether or not he should he tell him or just knock him out.

"She is in the hospital. She's in a coma."

"Who the hell is this?" Scott said, pointing at Adam's dead body.

"This is the guy responsible for putting Nyria in the hospital. Listen, Scott, I need your help. You have to trust me."

Scott raised his eyebrows.

"Oh no. I don't want anything to do with this. What hospital is she in?"

"You wouldn't know it if I told you."

"OK then, I'm calling the police. I knew there was a reason I didn't like you."

"Damn, you're hard-headed. Just like Nyria."

Sebastian had only one choice. Either the police show up and make things more difficult for him or pull Scott through the wall with him.

"Think, think, think!" Sebastian said.

Scott was pulling out his cell phone, getting ready to push 911. Sebastian grabbed the phone out of Scott's hand in one motion and placed his hand on the wall beside him, opening it to his realm.

Scott was in a daze. He could see the wall change to wavy lines. During his amazement, Sebastian flung Adam's body over his shoulder while grabbing on to Scott's arm and pulling them in.

They arrived in Newbia. Scott's eyes were as big as toonies, scouring the scenery. His mouth dropped. Everything was so bright and beautiful. Nothing could compare to it. The sky above them was light blue with a few clouds. The streets were clean. The roads were made of stone and the grass was even greener than home. It looked like a fairy-tale world.

The buildings were perfect. The cars were not of Scott's world. They looked the same, but something about them was different.

"Water, dude. They run off of water," Sebastian said, responding to Scott's curiosity.

"Where am I?"

"You are in Newbia. This is my world. This is where I come from. I will explain it to you later. We have to get going. Nyria is in trouble."

Nyria's name broke the spell covering Scott's curiosity.

"Nyria's here?"

"Yes, and like I told you, she's in the hospital. Oh, and, um, it is not actually Nyria in trouble. Well, she is, but our baby is too."

Scott almost chocked on his own spit.

"*What?* What baby?"

"I'll explain later, we have to go. Follow me."

As he ran toward the town square, he swung Adam's corpse to the ground near a garbage bin.

He glanced back at Scott every once in a while to make sure he was keeping up. Scott was a bit slower than he was, but he was staying with him nonetheless.

Turning a corner three blocks away, they entered the town square. Scott stopped abruptly and stared at all the warriors.

There were tens of thousands of them, some standing in the distance. Tyberrius was standing on a pier, preaching to them all.

"Today will be our day of victory, my follow Newbians. If we die, remember we die for the queen we've been longing for. Today we shall stand tall, together as one. *Today we fight!*"

They screamed loudly and raised their weapons, water pistols, swords and ropes, as they cheered.

Sebastian bolted through the crowd and took his place beside Tyberrius, roaring, "*To Lubria!*"

Their ships were docked at the end of the road. Issac approached Sebastian, giving him his best. Scott walked over, still mesmerized, wondering what was going on and why was he there.

As soon as Issac noticed him, he glanced toward Sebastian with curious eyes. Coming down off the pier, he waved Issac to follow him. As they approached Scott, Issac was the first to speak.

"Who is this? And why is he here?"

"Yeah, um, I was about to ask the same thing," Scott proclaimed, placing his arms across his chest.

"I had to bring him here. We need his help. Lubrians are weak and sneaky. There is a lot of them. The more willing to fight on our side the better our odds. Plus, he loves Nyria as I do. He will be of great help to us. I had no choice, he was going to call the police on me, making it more difficult than it needed to be. I was actually going back to Earth to get Kevin, but I ended up in Nyria's apartment."

Stopping to take a breath, Sebastian was now facing Scott with sarcasm in his voice. "Where I seem to recall you breaking her door in, knucklehead. Anyway, there's no time to explain; we have to get aboard a ship if we're going to leave with everyone. Are you with me, Scott?"

Scott had no idea what he was getting himself into but, he would do anything for me. I was like a sister to him.

"You have a lot of explaining to do on the way, wherever it is we're going, but I guess I'm in."

"Good, follow me," Sebastian said while en route, heading toward the last remaining ship.

As they entered, Tyberrius greeted Scott with a firm handshake.

"Welcome aboard, fellow earthling."

Tyberrius laughed.

"I've always wanted to say that."

As the ship lifted to the sky, neither Sebastian nor Scott knew what was in store for them. Tyberrius warned them to sit on the walls of the ship, as it was about to take off. They found a spot and sat with their backs up against the ship's interior.

Sebastian started explaining everything to Scott. Without warning, the ship soared faster than the speed of light through the sky, heading toward blackness.

Lubria was in eye's view. Besides that, there was nothing to see but space. Sebastian tried talking through the whole ordeal, explaining the whole story in a shorter version.

Scott's stomach was feeling the waves of the ride, but he kept his composure.

As they moved silently above Lubria, Sebastian's explanation came to an end. Scott was handed a water pistol and quickly shown how to use it.

The men stood up and looked out the back of the ship, adjusting their eyes to see through the darkness that covered Lubria. The smell was horrible.

They were high enough so that Lubrians walking below would not notice. They could see the tall structure from a distance, the building that held our child.

Sebastian motioned to Tyberrius—that's where they were headed.

War

The ship landed just outside the perimeter, where Lubrians dumped their garbage. They hid themselves amid the rubbish.

Tyberrius gave orders to the warriors to head out, splitting them into groups. Some went east and the others went west.

Sebastian was with the eastern group. He noticed Kevin Laung suited up to fight alongside him.

"Kevin? Long time no see."

"Yeah, well, I thought I would come and fight for my queen and the child. Lisa didn't want me to come, but we Newbians stick together. She's back on Earth. She wanted to come, but I told her she couldn't enter my realm pregnant or the baby would die. Women!"

"Oh, I see. Well, congratulations on becoming a dad," Sebastian said, hanging his head low.

Kevin could see the pain in his eyes, so he changed the subject.

"Who's this guy?"

"This is Nyria's best friend. It's a long story why he's here. No time to explain."

Two Lubrians walked around the corner. Shocked and surprised, they rang out, "Newbians!" and ran toward town.

"Get 'em!" Kevin shouted. But the Lubrians were fast creatures. They made it to the centre of town, yelling to warn everyone.

"Newbians are here! Newbians are here!"

Sebastian was not long behind them and he jumped on top of the two Lubrians, slashing their throats. But by then it was too late—everyone knew they were there.

Sebastian motioned to his comrades to follow him. He headed for their tallest building. Along the way they met up with Lubrians ready to battle.

Sebastian was the first to engage. His training had nothing to do with his ability to kill. He seemed to be indestructible. He was just another soul lost in the chaos.

Hate began to take over. He lost himself along the way. Darkness reigned over him.

"Get to know me!" he yelled while slashing throats, breaking necks and power-soaking them.

He was out of control. All that he could think about was our child and the deaths that would follow him as he walked through Lubria.

At one point he thought he was at his destination, but it was the wrong building. Lubrian warriors began to surround him. He glanced around before he broke loose. He danced around them as they circled him. He was ready to play.

"Let me feel your death!" he sang out. He killed the Lubrians one by one as they approached.

After slaying the last Lubrian, Kevin dashed to his side. Tyberrius and two other warriors came rushing in with their hands on their swords. The rage in Sebastian's eyes was unlike anything they'd ever seen. He was beginning to scare them a little.

Sebastian turned to his fellow Newbians, shouting, "I'm going to get Luther and Carmella alone. They are mine!"

Tyberrius stood with his chest swollen in protest.

"That's suicide, Sebastian. We never break formation."

"Today, Tyberrius, we do. They are the reason I am here. They took my child and they will die at my hands."

"Fine, but we're going in with you. You can have them to yourself. I promise."

They nodded in agreement and headed for the other tall building. As they entered, it fell quiet.

"Be careful, they might be lurking in the shadows," Tyberrius warned.

Scott was the last to enter. He was scared of the place. He had just killed creatures he thought were make-believe. Fear was creeping in on him. His legs were shaking and his hands were trembling. Sebastian noticed and hurried to his side.

"Scott, stay here and keep watch."

"No problem. I think . . . I'll stay here. Good idea."

Scott did surveillance of the area, just in case Lubrians were planning to attack them from the back, while Tyberrius, Kevin and Sebastian moved forward.

Sebastian was trying to remember what I had told him. He motioned to the door at the end of the hall, whispering, "That's where they are."

The three men were slowly approaching the door when Lubrian guards jumped from above. One landed on Kevin with a hard thud, knocking him unconscious.

Tyberrius power-soaked one of the Lubrians and watched him melt into slop.

Sebastian threw the other against the wall and stabbed a long spear into its heart.

They had to be more careful.

"They can crawl on the ceiling?" Sebastian asked.

"I guess so," Tyberrius mumbled.

Opening the door, they saw Luther holding our child in what looked like a large syringe.

"If you take another step forward, I will smash him to the floor."

Sebastian stiffened as the words fell off Luther's lips. He wanted to rush in and brutally kill Luther but, there was too much at stake

Carmella walked out from behind Luther, stealing the child from his grip. She whistled through the room as she glided away, threatening, "The child belongs to me. I will not let you hurt him."

Carmella seemed to have some type of love for our child. Was she helping the Newbians, or was this some type of trick?

As Carmella and Luther stared each other down, Sebastian moved slowly toward them. Carmella noticed his approach and quickly crawled up the wall and out of the window above, giving Sebastian a chance to move in on Luther while Tyberrius took off after Carmella.

Two Newbian warriors stood on guard at the door.

Sebastian now had Luther in his hands. Luther was unguarded.

He heard commotion coming from behind him. Sebastian turned to look while holding Luther in his grip. He watched the two warriors who stood confidently at the door die at the hands of Lubrian warriors.

He didn't let go of Luther, and got elbowed in the face. Luther had a few tricks up his sleeve.

He ran toward his guards, hiding behind them like a coward. Sebastian grunted, licking the blood off his lips and roaring in anger, "Show me how defenceless you really are, without anyone to hide behind!"

Tyberrius plunged into the room, knocking Luther and his guards to the ground. Sebastian came running over and grabbed Luther by the face, lifting him to his feet.

Tyberrius killed the guards with one swift blow to the back of the head. Rising to his feet, he put his hand on Sebastian's shoulder, uttering, "Luther is yours to finish, as promised. But I must tell you Carmella got away from me. Our warriors won't let her get far."

Sebastian's blood was boiling in his veins as Tyberrius gave him the news. His grip was stronger now. He placed his other hand on Luther's throat.

"I'll drown you in your own blood. Where did Carmella take my baby?"

Unable to talk, Luther shook his head back and forth in protest. Sebastian grew angrier. With his free hand, Sebastian gracefully slid his sword from its pocket chamber and whispered into Luther's ear, "Say goodbye as you dance to your death."

Luther was starting to suffocate. Death was dancing all around him. He felt nothing but pain as his neck bones were being crushed.

Before he took his last breath of life, Sebastian eased up on the force behind his hand, slashing Luther's insides with his sword, letting him submerge and drown in his own blood like he promised.

He stood over him, watching him die slowly, taking in the pleasure of Luther's death. Tyberrius rushed to his side.

"We have to get Carmella, Sebastian, let's go. He's dying, there's nothing more to do."

Sebastian moved stealthily toward the doors, on the search for Carmella. Finding Kevin still unconscious, he kicked his stomach, waking him from his sleep.

"Get up, Kevin, we must go!"

As Kevin stumbled to his feet, Tyberrius pulled him close and put his head under his arm for support. They jogged to where Scott was standing and ordered him to follow. The four of them walked out of the building to find Carmella standing with Newbian warriors.

"We found her, Sebastian. She was trying to flee, but we caught up with her," a warrior said, holding the syringe that contained our child.

Sebastian's heartbeat was irregular now. His anger was leaving him. He threw his sword to the ground and grabbed the syringe.

He gazed at the baby through the glass syringe and gently tucked it to his chest under his protective vest. He stared into Carmella's huge eyes, demanding, "Why? Why would you do this, Carmella?"

Carmella knew this was the end of the road for her, so she confessed.

"He is mine, not yours! He will bring nothing but good back into our realm. We meant no harm to him. Luther wanted him dead, but I want something different. I've seen what he could do for my people."

Taking a stance in front of Carmella, Sebastian roared in rage, "He will never belong to you! He is dying, you fool. He is not meant to be without his mother. You almost killed them and you will pay the price for that."

"No, please wait! I can help you. I know he is dying. But you see, I am the only one who can put him back where he needs to be. I will only help if you promise me something."

"I make no promises to Lubrians."

"You must, or he and your precious Nyria will die."

Sebastian knew she was right. But, he didn't want to promise her anything.

"What, what is it that you wish me to promise you?"

"When the baby is back inside of Nyria, you allow me to know him. Allow him to come back here to do good for my people. This is my wish. If you decide not to comply, I will not help you."

Sebastian grew angrier with her demands. Given all that had happened, he knew he had to make a deal with this Lubrian elder.

He would have to lie to get what he wanted.

"Agreed."

"Good, then. We should go, there's not much time. More Lubrian warriors will come," she warned him.

Tyberrius motioned to his warriors to shackle Carmella, and they fled to their ships.

Sebastian approached Tyberrius whispering, "I do not trust her. Make sure the warriors watch her every move. I need her help, but I will not be keeping my promise. Once she has done what she says, I will kill her myself."

Tyberrius nodded his understanding and agreed.

Reunited

Reaching the realm of Newbia, the warriors were beginning to feel comfortable. They souded their horns as they arrived in the town square. People came running out of their homes and stores to greet the warriors. Many froze when they saw the face of Carmella.

Her big black eyes stared at them as they glared. She didn't feel threatened being in their realm, she felt calm and submissive.

Sebastian rose and stood next to her to assure them she wasn't a threat to his people.

Irene was there waiting. Sebastian rushed to her, holding the baby who lay dying in the syringe. He leaned toward Irene, whispering, "Carmella is here to help you reunite Nyria with the baby. She said she can be helpful in putting the baby back where it belongs."

With half a smile, Irene replied, "Good, I need all the help I can get. I've never done this before."

Sebastian turned to the warriors who held Carmella and asked them to escort her to the hospital. They nodded and followed Irene to the ambulance waiting to take her back.

There wasn't time for chit-chat. Sebastian jumped in the front seat of the ambulance and drove with them.

Reaching the hospital, Sebastian was the first one out. He headed to the back of the ambulance to take Carmella to my hospital room.

Carmella took a deep breath as she approached my body.

"Has she been like this long?"

"Yes, since you took her."

"I see. Well, let's get started. We need to sterilize the room first. If you're going to stay, Sebastian, you need to get cleaned up as well."

Agreeing with her, he told Carmella to follow the warriors to the sanitizing room and that he would be there shortly. Irene had already gone to clean up.

Nurses came into the room and placed medical equipment around my bed for the operation. Sebastian leaned over me. He kissed my lips and whispered, "I love you, baby. Everything will be OK. The baby will be back inside you soon, my love. I'll be right here too."

Sebastian started walking toward the door. He saw Kevin entering the hospital.

"Kevin, what are you doing here?"

"I am here to make sure things were OK with you. I've known you all my life and I've never seen rage in your eyes like that before. I just wanted to be here if you need anything. I'm not going back to Lisa until the baby is back with Nyria. Plus, Lisa will want details. She's a tough one."

Understanding exactly what Kevin meant, Sebastian giggled to himself.

"Thanks Kevin . . . for everything."

"You don't need to thank me. I told you, Newbians stand by each other as one."

Sebastian smiled before heading to the sanitizing room. Meeting with Irene, Carmella, and two warriors guarding her, they all began sanitizing. After, they gowned up and headed to my room, where they would work together as a team to put the baby back into my uterus.

Sebastian was still holding our unborn child in its syringe. Slowly, when the time was right, he reached inside his gown and handed the baby to Irene.

"Please, Sebastian, stand out of the way."

He calmly stepped back to let them do their jobs.

He watched them carefully to make sure Carmella wasn't trying anything funny. He wasn't sure what they were doing, but he was curious enough to keep moving side to side, viewing every movement.

Irene and Carmella were working great together. One was asking the other to do certain things in compliance.

Removing the baby carefully out of the syringe, they injected it into a small tube. Irene cut a small hole in my bellybutton to give the tube enough room to enter. Carmella took the tube from Irene's hands and pushed it slowly into the incision. Watching the monitor, they connected the umbilical cord to my stomach.

They coated the outer layer of my uterus with some kind of foam.

"This is it. I think we've got it," Carmella announced while pushing the end of the tube straight up.

The baby was now back in my uterus.

They waited to see if the baby would move on its own to get comfortable, which it did.

They stitched the incision closed and covered it with a bandage so there would be no infection.

"Hooray!" they cried as they wiped the sweat from their foreheads.

Sebastian began hushing them all.

"Keep your voices down. I don't want to stress either of them out."

My hand twitched. Everyone in the room became still, staring at each other. They couldn't comprehend what just happened.

Before anyone could say a word, I opened my eyes.

"Nyria?" Sebastian cried. "Nyria, I'm here, sweetie."

I raised my hand up to Sebastian's face, touching him softly. Still weak, I fought to say, "I love you, Sebastian."

"I love you too, Nyria. The baby—"

"I know, I can feel it. It's happy now and in no more pain."

I glanced around the room while Sebastian covered me like a shield in battle, protecting its warrior.

I noticed Carmella. The same woman who had kidnapped me and tensed up. Sebastian felt my emotions. Colours filled the room. They were unlike the colours anyone had ever seen before. They were all mixed together.

Removing my hand from Sebastian's face, I moved it toward Carmella as if to tell her to take it.

She started to move toward me, but the guards stopped her.

"No, please, let her come to me."

Carmella was pleased. She smiled and slowly approached. She took my hand and something strange happened.

The room opened up with bright lights and colours that were clearer than ever. Carmella and I were glowing like the morning sun.

At certain moments, it was too bright to look at straight on.

"What's happening?" Sebastian questioned.

"She is our baby's protector, Sebastian."

"What? She is the one who took the baby from you, Nyria."

"Yes, but I know why she did it. She meant no harm to it. She thought it was best for everyone. Luther wanted it to die, but she kept it safe. I see it all clearly now."

Carmella's spirit was lifted by my words. Sebastian, on the other hand, was not convinced.

"Nyria, sweetheart," he said as he kneeled in front of me.

"Our baby . . . is a boy," he explained with cheer in his voice.

"A boy? How do you know this?"

"Well, sweetie, I'm sure you know about the birds and the bees. There is a long—"

"Oh, OK, forgot I asked."

Irene interrupted. "Sebastian, dear, Nyria needs to rest. The baby also needs silence in the room so he can adjust."

"OK, I will be back later to check on you. I will also have guards standing outside if you need me or anything, OK?"

I nodded, closed my eyes and puckered my lips. Sebastian leaned forward and placed a soft kiss on them.

He turned to escort Carmella out of the room. Irene was not long following. There were unfinished procedures.

Outside my door, Sebastian placed his hand on Carmella's shoulder.

"Thank you."

"No need to thank me. I will go home now, but I will be back when he is born, as per our agreement." Carmella said.

Sebastian clenched his teeth. He wanted to kill her, but he was grateful all the same. He smiled softly and agreed. He asked the guards to take her back to Lubria.

As she walked toward the front doors of the hospital, Carmella turned and waved at Sebastian, giving him a wide smile. Then she was gone.

Irene appeared from the room with gratitude written all over her face. She was happy and surprised at how well she and Carmella had worked together. She was a Newbian working alongside a Lubrian. She never thought in a million years this would ever happen.

"Go home, Sebastian. You need your rest. You can come back later, Nyria is resting now."

"OK. Will you give me a call if she wakes up?"

"Yes, I sure will."

Sebastian was still dressed in his hospital gown. He looked down at himself, unbuttoned it and threw it into a garbage can.

When he walked outside, he saw Kevin still hanging around.

"Hey Kev, everything went great!"

"Yeah, I know, I was talking to Carmella when the warriors took her out. She said something about her coming back here when the baby's born. Are you gonna stick to your agreement? I thought you said—"

Holding his hands out, Sebastian interrupted him.

"Nyria told us all that. Carmella is our baby's protector and she did help with her operation. I'll just wait and see what she wants from him when the time comes. I'm going home to get cleaned up and take a nap. Are you going back to see Lisa?"

"Oh, yes, she's probably pacing in her apartment right now."

Scott turned the corner, out of breath.

"Scott, you OK?" Sebastian asked.

"Yeah, I just ran all over this place trying to find you. Where's Nyria?"

"She is resting. The baby and her are fine. The doctor wants her to get some sleep, but you can come with me to get cleaned up. Then I will bring you back so you can see her, if you want."

"Yeah, that sounds good. I am starving, though."

"No worries, my mother is a great cook. She probably has food on right now."

Sebastian turned to Kevin and asked him if he wanted to join them. Kevin couldn't wait to see Lisa, so he thanked Sebastian and declined.

"OK guys, I will see you later. And Scott, good job back there. You need anything just let me know," Kevin said.

"Thanks, man. I'm good. I'm just waiting for Sebastian to fill me in on whatever is going on. I'm sure there's more. Nice place, though," Scott replied, being a little bit of a smartass.

Kevin left them standing there, staring into each other's eyes.

"All right, let's go," Sebastian told him.

"How are we getting there? No teleporting this time?"

Sebastian laughed. "No, we can walk if you like."

"Well, then again, I like the teleporting thing."

"Unfortunately we cannot teleport here in Newbia. We have to walk. Plus, it will give me time to explain things."

Scott agreed and they both began walking toward Sebastian's parents' house. Along the way, Sebastian told him about how Newbians, first people ever created, and how they made Earth to hide humans from the Lubrians.

He explained that Lubrians were the reason Newbian woman cannot have children, and that they took them and did experiments on them.

Scott interrupted at times to ask if he was also a seed. Sebastian told him that only women can be seeds. Men in Newbia can reproduce, but the women are sterile so there is no need for them to go to Earth.

He told him that once you live in Newbia you do not age like you would on Earth.

"Living here prolongs your life. The oldest Newbian here is 1,020. He has another ten years to go. Nyria will also live a long and prosperous life. And now that she is the queen, she will have more than enough happiness and love living here."

"Hey, now that you said she's the queen, how did that happen?"

"There is a legend that an Earth woman will get pregnant at the age of twenty-four and something will go wrong. She will then come to Newbia and conceive a child. Nyria is that seed."

"What does it matter that she is twenty-four?"

"Seeds can only get pregnant from a Newbian man at the age of twenty-six. Nyria is an exception."

"How old are you, Sebastian?"

"I'm twenty-four as well. Nyria and I were born at the same time. That's how it works."

"I get it. So why were you untying that guy's body in Nyria's apartment?"

As Scott asked his question, Sebastian's rage peeked through.

"He was the reason the Lubrians kidnapped her. He was also born at the same time as Nyria. Sometimes that happens. It's up to the elders to decided who will impregnate the seed. He didn't go to them to ask and neither did I because we didn't know we had the same seed. We eventually found out, but it was too late. He was a traitor. Anyone who is against us is our enemy and they must die. So now he's dead."

"Is there anything else?"

"Oh yeah, there's more. Nyria and I can read each other's emotions. I lost connection with her when she turned eighteen and we still don't know why. That is why I came to Earth two years before I was supposed to. The elders wanted me to find her to try and figure out why we lost our connection. They thought there was something wrong with me, but after doing six years of testing they found nothing."

"Maybe you lost connection with her because two of you were after the same seed."

"That could be so, but like I said, two Newbian men had the same seed before and they never lost connection at all. This is something different. Nonetheless, we are together now and no one will ever stand in the way . . . not even you, ya punk," Sebastian added as he ran up the dirt road to his parents' house.

Scott trailing behind him saying, "You only said that 'cause you were home. Come say that to my face."

Sebastian stop dead in his tracks.

Scott became a little bit intimidated and said, "I'm just kidding. Man oh man, you're a fighter, aren't ya?"

Scott giggled, but was still a bit afraid.

Sebastian smiled. He knew Scott was a little intimidated by him. He waved him into the house.

Going Home

After a good night's sleep and a lot of explaining, Scott learned about Newbia and its people.

With a full understanding of Newbia, they drove together to the hospital where they found me sitting up in bed, waiting for their arrival.

My room was full of balloons, flowers and cards sent by Newbian families.

"Hey, my two favourite boys," I said, not realizing I wasn't surprised to see Scott there.

"Nyria, baby, you're up. How are you feeling?"

Sebastian put his hands lightly around my cheeks and kissed my forehead. He lowered his head, avoiding eye contact. He couldn't take the chance of engaging me, not right after all that I'd been through.

"You don't have to lower your head at me, I can totally block now. And to answer your question, I'm feeling 100 percent better. I feel like new."

Scott slowly strutted to my bed and interrupted, turning into Mr. Smartass.

"Hey chick, long time no see, eh? Do you have any idea what we've been through? Better yet, we're in fucking la-la land. This shit is crazy. We're not on Earth no more," he announced, laughing between each sentence.

"No, but I know you're about to tell me."

I giggled. Scott's eyes grew wide as he continued.

"I fought these ugly Lubrians, and boy did I kick ass."

Laughing out loud, Sebastian interrupted Scott's story. He caught himself as my eyes glared at him. Scott rolled his eyes then continued once again.

"Like I was saying, I kicked ass! And we got this . . . I mean, your baby back. They operated on you last night."

I interrupted him.

"I know, somehow I felt and heard everything. Something I wanna ask, though. How long will I be pregnant? I mean, is it the same as a normal birth, or . . ."

Sebastian was quick to answer.

"Everything is the same, Nyria: pregnant for ten months. You go through all the same transitions. We are not all that different from you. We just live longer and we've learned to use our gifts."

"Gifts?"

I was puzzled. I thought I knew all there was to know about Newbians.

"Yes, you have gifts within you. Humans just find them hard to use. Some don't even know they have them. The way we feel each other's emotions are considered gifts. Seeds on Earth have the ability to feel the emotions of others, but they are so self-absorbed they don't realize it. But enough about that, sweetie, I just want you to get better so we can get you out of here and back at home."

"Home, as in Earth? 'Cause that's where I want to go, Sebastian."

I was trying to avoid hurting his feelings.

"Yes, Nyria, Earth. You're not supposed to be here until you're twenty-six, so we have another two years to stay on Earth, even though Newbians know who you are now. They take pride in their beliefs. They also know that when you return they will have to serve you as their queen. They are willing to wait."

Scott had to put his two cents in, course.

"Yeah, well, I go wherever you go, Nyria. I like it here. It is peaceful and beautiful, but it's not like home."

Sebastian and I looked at each other in amazement. Sebastian spoke first.

"Scott, you won't be coming back here. You're not supposed to be here in the first place. I needed your help and this is where it ends."

Scott was now standing in defensive mode, his arms firmly across his chest.

"So you used me? I'm only good for helping you and your band of skinny warriors . . . yeah, right. When Nyria comes back here in two years, my ass will be right alongside her, queen and all. You can call me King Scott."

"Scott, stop pestering Sebastian, will ya? You can't be king, ya fool. Sebastian will be king. You can be the jester."

Sebastian didn't like that I was taking Scott's side on coming back here to Newbia. It had never happened before. A regular human couldn't come here unless they were the seed of a Newbian. Scott was not one of them. But if I wanted him here he would not interfere with my decision. For I will be queen. Even though Sebastian would be king, the queen has the final say.

Irene walked into the room.

"OK, boys, Nyria has to have a physical now. Can we have the room to ourselves?"

Sebastian and Scott nodded in agreement. Before Sebastian left, he placed a kiss on my lips.

"I'll be right outside. When she's done I'll be back, OK?"

"Sebastian, I'll be fine."

He walked backwards out of the room with his eyes glued to me. Irene closed the door behind him.

He waited by the door while Scott wandered the hospital hallways, looking to see if there was anything different from his world to this one.

Six minutes passed and Irene opened the door.

"Sebastian? Could you come in here, please."

Sebastian was shocked to see me sitting at the end of the bed fully dressed in his mother's old clothes. She had brought them down for me to wear when I was released.

"What's going on? Why are you dressed?"

"She can go home, Sebastian. She has made a 360 degree turn for the better, and the baby is doing great. There is no need for her to stay here any longer," Irene explained.

Sebastian was overwhelmed by the news. He looked around the room to make sure I wasn't forgetting anything. He placed his strong hands around my waist for leverage to help me stand.

"Is there anything she should or should not do, Irene?"

"No, just the norm, I guess. Also, do your everyday stuff, Nyria. Oh, make sure she gets some prenatal vitamins and eats lots of healthy foods . . . no grease!" Irene explained, winking at me.

"Thanks, Irene. I appreciate everything."

"You're more than welcome, my queen."

"Please call me Nyria . . . just Nyria."

Sebastian slowly picked me off the ground and into his warm arms. He carried me out into the hallway and Scott appeared.

"What's going on? Is Nyria free to go?"

"I'm taking her home. Home as in Earth. And you're coming, Scott."

Scott was a little confused. He thought I was just having a physical, and now I was going home.

As we walked out the hospital doors, all the nurses waved at us, blowing kisses. I smiled and caught each one as they were thrown.

Scott raced to open each door to make it easier for Sebastian to manoeuvre me around the doorways.

"Scott, can you go get the car? The keys are in my right pocket."

Scott rummaged through Sebastian's pocket to find the keys. He dashed around cars to see where they had parked.

As Scott searched for the car, it gave us some time to talk.

"There has been a lot happening since you were been kidnapped and in a coma. But I think I will fill you in when you're home and more comfortable," Sebastian suggested.

"Yeah, can you tell me about it? There's been a lot happening within me, too."

Sebastian squinted his eyes, very confused from my statement.

"I mean, I know things I didn't before. I know what others are thinking and feeling, and their actions before they actually do them. Ever since the Lubrians took me."

Sebastian was utterly stunned. He didn't know what to say to that. He just held me close to him, peeking around my head to see where Scott was with the car.

Scott pulled up and leaned over to open the passenger door and Sebastian placed me into the seat. He shut the door and headed for the driver's seat.

Scott watched as he walked around the car. He had no intention of getting out.

"I'm driving, Scott."

"I could have sworn I was sitting here first."

"It's my mother's car."

"I don't care if it's the pope's car."

I shook my head at the two children arguing over who was going to drive. Why did we need a car to go back to Earth, I thought, before yelling at them.

"Stop it, the both of you! Scott, get out! Let Sebastian drive his parents' car. Be fair."

Scott sighed and got out of the driver's seat, mumbling under his breath. He almost shoulder-nudged Sebastian, but remembered what happened to his shoulder the last time.

Still huffing and puffing, he climbed into the back seat.

Sebastian took his place and waited for Scott to put his seatbelt on to drive off.

"My parents wanted to formally meet you before we go back to Earth. Plus, I'm sure they don't want me to leave their car at the hospital."

"Oh, that's right, your parents. Huh! They won't be upset for you not calling them first?"

Sebastian let out a hearty laugh.

"Are you kidding. They are going to love you. Plus, who wouldn't want to meet their queen? Just remember, none of us really knew about the legend our elders kept a secret. So they might call you queen instead of Nyria. Don't let that bother you, OK?"

I bit my bottom lip, a little nervous. I was about to meet my future in laws, and to make matters worse, I was their queen.

"Who would have thought," I mumbled to myself.

Scott was quiet in the back seat throughout the whole ride. He was mesmerized by the beauty Newbia had to offer.

I glanced out the windows once or twice at the beautiful scenery, but I kept my head down, staring at my belly, rubbing its smooth skin and making little circles around my incision. Sebastian watched from the corner of his eye, feeling grateful I was doing a lot better and that that our baby was doing great.

We pulled up to a little yellow cabin, where we saw Sebastian's mother Charlene standing in the doorway, waving franticly.

I smiled from ear to ear. This was the first time meeting Sebastian's parents. Well, while I was conscious, anyway.

From a distance, Sebastian resembled his mother.

Sebastian unbuckled my seatbelt and jumped out of the car to open my door. Scott made it there before him. He placed an arm under me for support.

"I can get her, Scott, Thanks."

Scott paid no attention to him and he gently lifted me out of the car and into his arms. Sebastian trailed behind us, kicking the dirt in frustration.

"Oh, Sebastian," his mother cried wrapping her arms around his neck. "Please bring her to the living room where she will be more comfortable."

Scott manoeuvred around Sebastian and his mother, laying me on the loveseat that sat in the corner of the room.

I was checking out my surroundings, when my eyes grew wide at the pictures of Sebastian on the wall. He was a little boy in most of them. One family picture hung above me. I bent my head back to gaze at it.

"Awww, I like this one of you, Sebastian."

Scott took the seat next to me and placed his arm over the back of the loveseat, making himself right at home. He smiled at Sebastian. I could see him snarling at Scott.

Sebastian was so pissed off, he didn't even introduce his mother to me. The room felt cold for a moment, until Charlene spoke, breaking the silent stare-down between Sebastian and Scott.

"I'm Sebastian's mother, Charlene. It's so nice to finally meet you. I was at the hospital with you, but you were in a coma so you don't remember me."

"Well, I knew you were there somehow. So it's nice to put a face to my feelings. Nice to meet you, too."

Sebastian was still in a staring match with Scott, even when he sat on the sofa adjacent to us. Charlene and I paid no attention to either boy until Sebastian's father walked in. All eyes stared at the tall, muscular figure.

"Hello, Nyria, my name is Bruce. I'm sure Sebastian told you all about us," he said, giving Sebastian a hard look to stop his ridiculous behaviour.

"A little. I feel like I already know you all."

Bruce walked firmly toward Scott and asked him to grab the blanket flung over a railing next to the loveseat.

Scott obliged and got up to retrieve it, and Bruce took the seat next to me. Scott didn't say anything, just took a seat on the sofa next to Sebastian. Sebastian grunted a little under his breath.

"Why didn't you give him any fuss?" Sebastian whispered to Scott.

"Whatever, man," Scott replied, shaking it off.

Charlene was in the kitchen fetching drinks and finger food. There was a lot of conversation between me and Bruce, while the two boys sat still listening to our conversation.

Charlene was back and forth, grabbing napkins and cups. She seemed to never sit down. Sebastian had to somehow break the news to his parents about taking me back to Earth as soon as possible. But he had respect for his elders when they were talking. He didn't want to interrupt.

He found the chance when I took a drink.

"Dad? I have to take Nyria back to Earth tonight."

His mother finally stopped walking back and forth and stood with her mouth open. His father shifted his weight toward him.

"Why tonight, son?"

"Well, we do have rules, Dad, that I'm not willing to break. Plus, her friends and family are probably wondering where she is. She has been missing for some time now and no one that I know of went back to erase their memories of her. We need to make sure they never find out where she was or that she was even gone."

Scott was on Sebastian's side on this one.

"Yeah, and Karen is probably going crazy 'cause you haven't shown up for your shifts. She most likely called the cops and put out a missing person's report. She's like a mother figure to you, Nyria."

"I have to agree with them too, Nyria," Bruce said with disappointment in his voice. "But they're right. Your family is probably worried by now."

"I have no family," I said as I hung my head down wanting to cry, but I held my tears back.

Sebastian felt my mood switch from happy to sad. He crept to my side and his hands gripped my knees.

"What is wrong, sweetie, did we upset you?"

"No. It's just that . . . Scott, Lisa and Karen are my only family and friends. My parents died on my eighteenth birthday. They were in a car accident. So the only person looking for me or even worried about me is Karen. She already lost her daughter Emily. I can't imagine what's going through her head right about now. You're right, we have to get back."

Sebastian's thoughts were going a mile a minute.

"I get it! I understand why we lost connection now."

I had no clue what he was talking about, but humoured him anyway.

"What?"

"We lost connection because you were going through a crisis and I have never been through anything remotely close to that. So, my feelings and emotions were all a scramble. It makes sense now. You were eighteen when they died?"

"Yes, my eighteenth birthday, to be exact."

"This is something Newbians have never faced before. I must tell them."

Bruce was convinced Sebastian was right, but this was not the time to run off to tell the elders of his findings.

"Sebastian, my son, I will tell the elders what we have learned here. You must take Nyria back to Earrth. That is more important right now, don't you think?"

Sebastian agreed. He was being sidetracked without noticing.

"Well, Dad, Mom . . . I love you and I guess I will see you in about two years."

"You can always come home to visit, Sebastian," Charlene cried.

"Yes, I know, Mom, but I need to stay with Nyria at all times now. I don't trust those Lubrians, even though Carmella helped us. They are still our enemies. And bringing Nyria along isn't the safest thing to do. We still are not sure the baby can handle going through realms. So it's best to say I will be back in two years. It's not a long time, Mom."

Charlene buried her face in her husband's chest. His father held out his hand to shake his.

"You take good care of her, and yourself. We love you. As for you, young lady, our queen of Newbia, we love you too," Bruce added.

Scott was feeling a little left out, so he strolled over and said, "No love for me I see. It's all good."

Bruce, still holding Charlene in his arms, grabbed Scott's shirt and pulled him in, giving him a hug.

"We love you as well, Scott. Who wouldn't?"

Bruce laughed, being a little sarcastic himself.

Charlene broke out of Bruce's grip and gave me a hug and kiss before she left the room crying.

"Mom . . ." Sebastian called after her.

"Let her go, son. She needs time to herself right now. Take care and we will see you soon."

Sebastian sighed as he lifted me off the loveseat and into his arms. He placed his palm on the wall beside him, opening the realm to Earth. He took one last look behind him and gave his father a soft, heartbreaking smile, then we were gone.

Scott soon followed, but not without saying thanks and goodbye.

The Myth

With my eyes closed we entered my apartment.

"Oh my god, what's that smell?" I yelled out, holding my breath.

Sebastian had forgotten to come back to clean the blood.

"Oh, right . . . well, it's a long story."

He had a lot of explaining to do, but the first thing was to get me comfortable. Sebastian darted to my bedroom, Scott gliding behind him.

"How are you gonna explain this one, Sebastian?"

Before Sebastian could answer, I questioned him myself.

"Yes, I'd love to hear the story."

I could see he didn't want to answer my question right away, so he changed the subject.

"Nyria, sweetie, I will clean the kitchen first. Stay here in your bedroom with Scott and I'll be back as soon as I'm done. Unless you wanna help me, Scott?"

"No thanks, man, it's all yours. I'll chill out with my homegirl. Have fun!"

Sarcasm never grew old with him.

Sebastian rolled his eyes and headed for the kitchen. He cleaned up pretty quickly. He was back in no time.

Scott was lying next to me, rubbing my belly, talking to the baby. "Gaga goo ga."

"That suits you, Scott."

Sebastian was getting this sarcasm thing down pat. I let out a good hearty laugh.

"He got you on that one, Scott, you have to agree."

"Whatever. So please tell us the story, old wise one. Why was there blood everywhere?"

Scott had to top Sebastian's sarcasm. He knew what happen, he was just being an ass. As usual.

Before Sebastian began, he softly lay beside me on the bed with his head tilted downward.

"Well, after you were kidnapped I went to Newbia for help. I came back here and things were out of place. There were dirty dishes left in your room. I knew I didn't do it. I heard your door opening and saw Adam, the guy you told me about from the diner. Well, he's a Newbian. You were his seed too, Nyria. Sometimes that happens. Unfortunately, he told the Lubrians about you and they came here to kidnap you. He confessed everything to me before I killed him. Then Scott knocked at your door and he saw Adam's body tied to the chair. I had to tell him what was going on and that's why Scott ended up coming to Newbia with me to fight for you and our baby."

I stared at him for a moment before realizing he had killed someone.

"I thought you said that if you kill someone here on Earth you will be killed when you return to Newbia."

"That is correct. You were the one who stopped them from killing me, Nyria."

"I was? How?"

Now holding my hand and staring deeply into my eyes, he replied, "When you were in the ambulance, you asked for me before you slipped away into a coma. The elders have to listen to whatever you say, so they let me go."

"Oh, I see. Well, I knew there was something fishy about that guy Adam. He was so upset when you sent those flowers to me."

Scott was dozing on and off as Sebastian and I were conversing. I leaned over to him, shouting, "You tired, Scott?"

His eyes grew big before answering me.

"Yeah! Do you mind if I crash right here?"

"No, go ahead. I'm not tired. Am I able to go to the kitchen now, Sebastian?"

Smiling, he leaped up off the bed and positioned himself in front of me with his hands out and waited for me to take them.

"Yes, it's all cleaned. You might smell strawberry spray, though. I found it under your sink."

"Well, at least I won't smell rotten blood."

Slowly I rolled out of bed as Sebastian gracefully helped me up.

"I'm OK Sebastian, really. I need to move on my own, please. Thank you, but I got it, sweetie."

He stepped back slowly, keeping enough distance just in case I needed his help.

A message came to him. "Nyria, sweetheart, the elders are coming here to talk to us."

Before it was Lubrians in disguise. I had to be sure these were the real elders of Newbia.

"Are you sure it's Newbian elders this time?"

"Yes, I will be on guard and Scott's here to help if we need him. But I think we'll be OK."

Nodding my head, I slowly sat down on the sofa. The wall quickly became wavy. The Newbian elders floated through with big smiles on their faces. Issac was the first to enter, followed by Jules, Amy, then Luc. All four were now standing in my apartment.

"Please have a seat." Sebastian gestured as he grabbed a few chairs from the kitchen.

Jules sat next to me on the sofa, placing her hands on top of mine.

"How are you feeling, Nyria?"

Jules had a soft spot for me.

"I feel good, thanks."

"Good. We are here to talk about the crisis you had at the age of eighteen, when your parents died. Bruce told us right after you left Newbia."

I knew I would have to fight the tears back as soon as I began. But nevertheless, I told them my story.

"Oh right. Well, like he probably told you, it was my eighteenth birthday and I got a phone call from my aunt, telling me both my parents were in a car accident. They were on their way home with my birthday cake."

Tears were running down my face. Sebastian sat on the other side of me with his arms wrapped around my waist, letting me know it was OK.

Jules continued. "So, let me understand, this all happened the day you turned eighteen. Well, I guess we know why you and Sebastian lost connection. You were unstable. We have had situations where seeds have gone through a traumatic ordeal. But they've always seemed to come out of it. I guess you were one of the few. How did you cope?"

Jules was holding my hands tightly as she felt the pain running through my body.

"My best friends, Scott and Lisa, they were there for me, through everything. If it wasn't for them, well . . ."

"You don't need to say it, Nyria. You're still here," Sebastian whispered in my ear, kissing my earlobe.

The room fell quiet as they all stared at me. Sebastian had the perfect chance to ask his question.

"There is something else I would like to ask you, my elders."

Everyone turned in his direction.

"When Nyria was in Newbia, she seemed to know everything . . . I mean, she knew what was going to happen and who was there when it was happening. But she was not conscious, or even in that area at each moment. Sorry if I'm not making sense, but none of it makes sense to me."

The elders sat straight up in their seats. The hair on the back of Luc's neck stood up straight. He cleared his throat.

"There is a myth that—"

Issac cut him off in mid-sentence. "I don't think it is necessary, Luc."

Luc changed his posture, and in a demanding voice he spoke again. "Well, I believe it is. They should hear about it. It might not be a myth at all. Look at what we've found out so far. She has made our legend come true. Why can't this be true as well?"

With his arms folded across his chest, he allowed Luc to continue. "OK, if you wish." He gave him the incentive, but still continued to be unhappy about his choices.

Luc said, "The myth is of a Newbian who knows the past and the future. He or she is called the All-Knowing Child, the heart of the realms. The myth has it that in 2014 the universe will explode into one. All that is in it will see the All-Knowing Child, and everything it creates will be everlasting. Maybe Nyria is the everlasting child, or her unborn."

Sebastian gasped for air before he added his conclusion.

"That's the reason Carmella said our baby will help their people. They want him to keep their world from dying too. Our baby is Nyria's and my creation, the everlasting child. Therefore, whatever is created by our baby in the future will never die either. They know about the explosion that will happen in 2014. With him, they don't have to worry about death."

My eyes were a glaze. "It makes sense," I added.

"They want him, and you will have me. No! They will never have my baby!"

Issac quickly planted his feet.

"So, the legend and the myth are true. We need to let our people know right away. The time will come when we all will have to face the Lubrians. They will not take kindly to us forbidding them to have your son. Come, my siblings, we must go and spread the word. Sebastian, keep Nyria close. Don't let her out of your sight. We cannot trust the Lubrians. If this is all true, we are in for a bigger war than ever before."

The elders gestured with a smile toward me as they headed to the wavy wall Luc had made for them. Jules took one last look at me before she walked through, saying, "If you need me for anything, send me a message and I will be there. Oh, and before I forget . . . everyone here on Earth who knows you will not remember that you're missing. I took care of that before we came, so please do not mention your disappearance to anyone, for they will not know what you're talking about."

I took a deep breath and smiled in agreement.

Then they were gone.

I couldn't wrap my head around this. It did not seem real. None of it.

"Please tell me this is all a dream. You're not real, right?"

I asked while grabbing Sebastian's arm, "I'm sorry, Nyria, it's not a dream. This is real. I know this can be a lot to take in, but I promise you, I will never let anyone take you or our baby boy ever again. They will have to kill me first."

"Please, no more. I want to talk to Scott."

I got to my feet. I stumbled a little, but Sebastian caught me before I ended up on the floor.

"Nyria, you have to rest."

"I know. Just let me talk to Scott, I will rest beside him. Can you give us a minute or two, please?"

Sebastian hated me confiding in Scott. He knew I told him everything. Sebastian wished I would confide in him instead. I felt his emotion drop to his knees. I turned to him and kissed his soft lips, moving my face away slowly.

"It's nothing personal, Sebastian, he just—"

He placed his finger over my lips.

"I will never question you, Nyria. If you want to talk to him in private, I respect your wishes. I will be in the kitchen making something for you to eat."

I rubbed his cheek, broke out of his grip and slid across the wall toward my bedroom.

Closing the door behind me, I noticed Sebastian's disappointed face and the slouch in his back as he turned the kitchen light on.

I just wanted to talk to my best friend.

"Scott, wake up."

I shook him like a rocket ship.

"What! What happened?" he roared as he jumped out of bed, almost knocking me to the ground.

"Gosh . . . I just need to talk to you. I'm OK. Just listen to me."

Scott was all ears. His eyes were bloodshot and he had bed lines across his face. I giggled at his appearance than continued.

"While you were sleeping, the elders came here to talk to me and Sebastian."

"And you didn't wake me?"

"Shut up and listen, please. They told us about a Newbian myth. Something about a Newbian knowing everything, called an All-Knowing Child, the heart of the realms. The everlasting! They think it's me. They also said that whatever I create will be everlasting too."

Scott's expression was similar to mine when the Newbian elders told me the story.

"OK, let me understand what the fuck you're talking about. They think you're some type of all-knowing child who will never die? Please tell me this shit is not true. What next? I swear we live in some crazy times."

I hated how everything seemed to end up as a joke with him.

"Do you always have to make a joke out of everything, Scott? I'm serious. I'm scared!"

He reached over and gave me a hug and a kiss.

"You know something, chick? I swear as long as I'm with you and that Joey . . . I mean, Sebastian, is with you, you don't have to be scared. I sort of like the guy and I know he loves you, and so do I. Don't worry, you're not alone. Don't be scared. What else did they say?"

"They also said that the universe will explode into one."

"What? OK, they have to be drug addicts, for sure. The world isn't going to explode."

Making myself more comfortable on the bed, I crossed my arms in protest.

"I wouldn't say that, Scott. Did you ever think in a million years something like this would ever happen? To you or anyone else, for that matter?"

"You got a point there. Are they gonna take you somewhere so you're safe?"

"They didn't say. They just left and told Sebastian to never let me out of his sight."

Sebastian was in the kitchen cooking chicken and rice while Scott and I were talking.

He was trying to tap into my emotions, but felt nothing.

Is she that good at blocking me, or are we losing our connection again like before? Sebastian thought to himself.

As he stood staring off into space, he began to feel my emotions stir up. They were still a blur, but readable. They felt scared, worried and confused. He knew I needed to take my mind off of everything.

He stopped staring into space; I was now exiting the bedroom. My eyes were a bit red from crying.

"Nyria, sweetie, why don't you get some sleep. You can lay in my arms all night and I will sing to you. Plus, I want to take you somewhere tomorrow, but you need to rest first."

Scott came out of the room.

"That sounds really good. Can I come too?"

"No, I would like to spend some time with her alone, if you don't mind."

Scott would agree, but not before barking orders first.

"OK, but you have to tell me where you're taking her."

Sebastian shook his head as if Scott was kidding. But he knew he was as serious as can be. He moved toward Scott, whispering in his ear, "If you want to come you can. Keep a distance, though. I'm not positive that the Lubrians won't try something funny again. I'm taking her to Rainbow Heaven Beach. I will have a lobster dinner there with candles and—"

"OK, OK. That's enough info. Geez, she's like my little sister, man."

I giggled before interrupting the two of them.

"All right, Sebastian, I will try and get some sleep."

Before I headed back to my bedroom, I leaned toward Scott's face and gave him a kiss goodnight.

"I'll be back in the morning, OK, Nyria. I just need to get some things from my place. I think I might move in or something."

Sebastian let out a long laugh.

"As if!"

Placing my hand on Scott's chest, I wished him a good night.

"Goodnight Nyria . . . oh, and night-night, pretty boy."

Sebastian opened the apartment door before uttering goodnight to Scott.

Rainbow Heaven

orning came quick. Sebastian's lullaby must have put me to
sleep faster than I thought.

"Good afternoon, sleepyhead."

"Afternoon?"

I peeked at the clock: 1:45 p.m.

"Why did you let me sleep so long?"

I was now sitting straight up in bed, a bit pissed at him for
letting me sleep half the day.

"You were tired, Nyria. Plus, you need a good night's sleep. I
didn't want to wake you. You looked so comfortable."

After listening to him, my attitude changed.

"Yeah, you're right, I was comfortable. I don't even remember
you singing to me."

He laughed under his breath. He had sung to me for no more
than five minutes. I fell asleep as soon as he held me in his arms.
But he wasn't about to tell me that.

"OK, you need a shower, my cute little queen. We are going
out for lunch. I know you're probably hungry. The baby is for
sure," he whispered while sliding his hands over my belly and
around my back, placing a kiss on my forehead.

"OK, but I'm taking a bath instead."

"Whatever you wish. Come, I'll run the water for you."

He untangled himself from me and gliding me to the bathroom, turning the water on, making it warm.

"Thank you, Sebastian. You're too good to me, you know that?"

"You have no idea how good I can be to you. We have a long life ahead of us and I will make you the happiest Newbian queen ever."

He unbuttoned my tank top, stylishly staring into my eyes.

"Stop that!"

I giggling. I wanted him to take me right then and there, but he was a bit rough when it came to lovemaking. I didn't want him to hurt the baby.

"If you're worried about me being rough, you can control that, you know," he mentioned, still trying to remove my top.

"Well, I am a bit worried, you're right. How can I control what you do?"

"Well, you're really good at blocking me. Maybe you need to block how much power I have behind thrusting you."

Blocking his stare was easier than blocking the words coming out of his mouth. He was turning me on just talking about thrusting me. The feeling I got when we were making love was out of this world, nothing anyone could ever explain.

"If you want to have lunch, Sebastian, I need to take a bath, so stop trying to seduce me," I suggested, a bit serious but tempted to let me win her over.

"OK, take a bath. I'll be waiting."

I blew him a kiss while closing the bathroom door. I lowered myself into the tub, enjoying the water running down my feet.

Ten minutes later I opened the bathroom door and wobbled to my long dresser beside the closet, asking him if I should wear something formal or casual.

"Casual."

I threw on a white sundress with yellow flowers swirling around the back and tying up around my neck. My belly was protruding from underneath it.

Grabbing my white flip-flops, I slowly danced out of the room.

Sebastian was lost for words. I was absolutely gorgeous. My hair was up in a ponytail with strands falling around my face. His pearly whites were gleaming. I moved closer to him.

"You are so beautiful."

The sincerity in his voice made me blush.

"Thank you. You're not so bad yourself."

I didn't know what to say. He had caught me off guard. He was more than "not so bad," he was a heartbreaker. Nothing and no one could ever compare to him or his personality.

"Shall we?"

Holding his hands out to me with a sexy look in his eyes, I moved forward, locking my hands into his.

"Yes, we shall. Oh wait, Scott didn't come yet, did he?"

The sexy look disappeared as soon as I uttered Scott's name.

"I called him and he said he would meet us back here at seven p.m."

"How did you get his number?"

I knew I hadn't given it to him.

"It's on your fridge, Nyria."

"Oh, right. Duh!"

He opened the door and peeked out before we went into the hallway, making sure it was clear to go. He couldn't take any chances.

I slowly walked out and waited for him to lock up. Hand in hand, we danced out of the building, where I saw his BMW waiting by the curb.

"How?"

"Scott went and picked it up for me. Nice guy, just a little goofy."

Laughing, Sebastian opened the passenger-side door and helped me in, and hurried to the driver's side.

Turning the air conditioning off that Scott had on full blast, we headed for Rainbow Heaven Beach.

Arriving at our destination, Sebastian asked if it was OK for me to be blindfolded. When I agreed, he wrapped a red scarf around my eyes. He was prepared for everything. With Scott's help, of course.

He leaped out and ran to the passenger side, opening my door. He guided me out with my hand in his. He wrapped his arm around my waist, slowly moving across the hot sand. He scoured the area, looking for Scott.

He saw him parked in the tall grass singing to himself. They made eye contact and Scott gave a smile. Feeling content, he removed my blindfold.

I slowly opened my eyes to find a white blanket spread across the sand with four stones holding it down at each corner. There was a small fire pit with a large silver pot hanging over it. Candles surrounded the blanket, buried deep into the sand, with glass shields covering them from the warm wind.

Written in the sand around the blanket were the words "I love you."

I couldn't hold back the tears any longer. I wept as I stared into his eyes.

"This is beautiful, Sebastian. I don't know what to say."

"Just say you're happy."

With one hand behind my back and the other holding my hands together, he carefully helped me sit in the middle of the blanket.

I could see people in the distance swimming and running in and out of the water. We were hidden from them by the tall grass growing around the shore.

"What's in the pot, Sebastian?"

"Lobster!"

My eyes grew wide and my mouth began to water.

"Yummy, my favourite," I said.

"Mine too, remember?"

"Yes, how could I forget."

He kneeled down, uncovered the steaming lobster and placed them on plates that had been sitting next to the fire pit.

He allowed them to cool while he poured red wine for himself and red Kool-Aid for me.

"I bought you red punch, since you can't have alcohol."

"Thanks, this is perfect."

Still kneeling, he passed me my glass and lay his down beside him.

Crushing the lobster's shell, he removed it. He dug out the sweet meat and prepared our plates with scallops and muscles, already cooked and sitting in a glass dish.

"This is yours, my love," he whispered, kissing me as I took my plate from his hand.

"Thank you."

Passing a napkin and fork to me, we began to eat, staring into each other's eyes, listening to the waves crashing on the shoreline.

"After you're done, do you think you can go for a short walk?"

"I'd love to. I can't remember the last time I walked along the ocean shore. This is amazing."

His face lit up like a Christmas tree.

"I'm glad you like it. This is what's in store for you, every day for the rest of your life with me. Your happiness is my happiness."

Finishing our food, we drank the rest of the wine and Kool-Aid. Sebastian jumped to his feet and felt his pocket.

"You ready?"

"Ready!"

He held his hand out for me to take. Slowly, he eased me to my feet.

"This belly of mine seems to weigh me down, eh?"

"I think you're cute. I wanna squeeze you, but I won't," he quickly assured me.

Walking in the warm sand, we reached a bunch of boulders.

"Please sit, Nyria. I want to ask you something."

As I stretched my arms behind me, reaching for a rock to sit on comfortably, he took hold of me and guided my body gently down, where I sat with my feet buried in the sand.

He took a deep breath and kneeled in front of me, saying, "No one will ever make me as happy as you have, Nyria. I've known you since birth. Even though we lost connection when you turned eighteen, I still think our connection is stronger than before. When I kiss your lips, you take my breath away. You're like a dream come true. You're the only one for me. I want to please you in every way. Anything you ask, I will do. I want to make you happy. All my life, I waited for this day and I am thankful that I finally found you. From the bottom of my heart, I'll love you the way you're supposed to be loved. Will you marry me?"

Tears of joy ran down my face as the lump in my throat grew bigger and bigger.

"Yes, I will marry you."

He retrieved a ring from his pocket and placed it on my finger. He was trying his hardest to hold back from breaking into tears, but it was coming no matter how hard he tried. The tears poured down his face and onto my sundress. I grabbed his face, bringing it closer to mine.

"I'm so glad I'm your seed. I love you more than words could ever say."

Kissing him, the sky opened up and colours filled the horizon—pinks, blues, reds and greens danced like birds soaring through the air.

People on the other side of the beach were gazing at the sight. Some were even taking pictures.

Scott got out of his car to glare at the skies.

It was beautiful, and it was all for us.

Planning

Arriving home, Scott pulled up behind us.

"Guess what, Scott?"

Rushing out the car and holding my belly, I continued. "Sebastian and I are getting married!"

Excitement was written all over my face. I jumped up and down like a kid with a new bike. I held out my left hand, showing off the diamond he had given me.

"I already know. He asked for my permission."

Suddenly, the excitement turned into confusion.

"Your permission?"

"Yeah, well, I'm the only other man in your life, right? He's supposed to ask your father for your hand in marriage, but since he's not . . . well, you understand, right?"

Sebastian was smiling as he emerged from the parked car. As he approached me, he locked his fingers around mine.

"I asked him out of respect. I knew he'd be pissed if I didn't. I'm getting to know him better with each passing day." He sounded as if he was getting tired of seeing Scott day in and day out.

I didn't know what to say. Both my best friend and soon-to-be husband were getting along. Scott was not being a jackass for once.

I gave them both a smile and a wink, and headed for the building doors.

"Come on, boys, it's time to prepare for the wedding."

Still smiling, I opened the doors, wobbling with excitement.

I could tell that Sebastian and Scott were not sure what I meant by telling them to prepare for the wedding. But they knew me well enough that they were sure it would be something to remember.

Dropping my apartment keys on the counter, I opened my phone book to call Lisa.

When she answered and I told her the news, she started screaming with joy and giving me wedding ideas. I had to find a chance to break her babbling.

"Lisa, Lisa, would you be my maid of honour?"

"Hell yeah! Oh, great. I'm gonna look huge in my dress." She sounded excited then disappointed. I too would have the same bump in front of me.

"Look at it this way, Lisa, we're gonna look like two pigs in a blanket."

I laughed out loud as I continued to wink at my boys, who were watching me pacing the kitchen floor. Scott took a seat while looking distastefully at Sebastian.

"I'm gonna watch TV. You wanna join me, Joey?"

"Sure, jackass."

Scott's expression was still. He didn't budge at Sebastian's remark. They sat apart from each other on the sofa, each at one end.

Clicking the TV on, there was a CBC broadcast: "Top news. Today a woman claims to have been abducted by aliens."

"If they only knew," Scott mumbled.

Sebastian gave a giggle before he turned to watch me pacing back and forth.

As I said my goodbyes to Lisa, he quickly turned back around, thinking I didn't notice.

"OK, Lisa is my maid of honour," I managed to say before to dialling another number.

"Who are you calling now?" Scott asked, looking at me from the coner of his eye while still bewildered by the television.

"Karen, of course. She would be upset if I didn't have her in my wedding. Plus, she would have loved to see her own daughter get married. She'll have the chance through me. I know she won't remember it, but I will."

Sebastian grew happier seeing that I had accepted the fact that I would have to leave Earth one day to go to Newbia with him.

"Is there anything you need me to do, Nyria?" Sebastian asked as he climbed out of his seat.

"No, Sebastian, thanks anyways."

I continued dialling Karen's number, while winking at him and biting my bottom lip.

"Hello, Karen?"

That was the only two words both men heard before the screaming started. Overexcited wasn't the word. I had a high tone in my voice as I talked with her.

It was exciting to have everyone else so happy. I was even happier when I got off the phone.

"Done! Oh, right we have to ask your parents and the elders, hon," I suggested, plopping down into his lap.

Caressing my back as he kissed my shoulders, he moved toward my ear, saying, "They already know, sweetie. I told them I was going to ask you. Jules was the first one to say she will be there. Just give her the date. We all sort of knew you would want to get married on Earth, since all your friends are here. We just have to give them a date and time. Mom and Dad will come and help if you need them to."

My cheeks were hurting from the smile on my face. It was growing bigger and bigger as the words fell off his soft, plush lips.

"Well, I'd love for your mother to help me. Plus, it's a good way to get to know her. She will be my mother-in-law soon. OK, but Sebastian, where are they gonna stay? There's no room here in this small apartment, especially with Scott here."

I was happy Scott came to stay with us for a while. Sebastian, on the other hand, wasn't too pleased. But as long as I was happy

Sebastian would do anything for me. That even meant putting up with Scott.

Scott cleared his throat before adding, "They can stay at my place. I paid rent to the end of the month, and since I'm staying here they can have it."

That was a great idea, but Scott wasn't staying here any longer. Sebastian and I needed time alone.

"Why don't you go stay with them, Scott?" Sebastian remarked, waiting impatiently for Scott to agree.

"Naw, I like it here better," he said, giving Sebastian that slyest wink.

I had to intervene.

"That sounds like a good idea, Scott. You should stay with Sebastian's parents at your place. That way they won't be lonely over there at night. You all will be here most of the time anyway. Plus, I'd like to have some alone time with my husband-to-be."

Scott crossed his arms in protest, but not before being a smartass again.

"Oh, you mean so you can get your freak on without his parents or me around. I getcha," he announced, winking at me then continuing to be a jerk.

"Plus, Joey here will like that too."

I had to put my foot down with this foolish name calling.

"Stop it Scott, be nice. Stop calling him Joey. You know his name."

Like a child, he stomped his feet while whining, "He called me jackass!"

Sebastian stood solid, his eyes rolling from side to side.

"I only called you jackass because you keep calling me Joey."

"Stop it, the both of you. You are acting like kids. I'm pregnant with moods swings and the two of you are worse."

Both of them realized I was right, and each said sorry and hung their heads in shame.

"Thank you, Sebastian. Let your parents know they can come a week before the wedding to help. I don't want anything big, just a few people. You know where we should get married? The Dartmouth Commons. It's so beautiful there this time of year."

Sebastian sighed, as he didn't know a whole lot about Nova Scotia and its surroundings.

"Where's the Dartmouth Commons? I'm not familiar with places in Nova Scotia, or anywhere on Earth for that matter."

"It's down by the waterfront, Joey . . . Sebastian."

"Thanks jackass . . . Scott," Sebastian uttered before thanking me.

"That sounds great, sweetie. Do we have to ask for permission to use that area?"

"No, it's open to the public. How about at the end of the month? That gives us three weeks to get everything ready."

"Whatever makes you happy, I'm happy with. The end of the month it is," Sebastian agreed before kissing my forehead.

Before the Wedding

"I think Scott's been driving my father insane these past couple of days."

I wasn't surprised at all. Scott always got under people's skin, no matter what the situation.

"Why do you say that?"

"Because they can't wait to stay here when I go there for the night. Which reminds me, tell me why I can't be with you the night before we get married again?"

"It's tradition. Plus, I don't want you to see me in my dress. That's bad luck."

"Oh, I see. What if—"

"No! Now get everything you need and be gone with you."

I chuckled and helping him gather his things. He didn't want to upset me, especially the day before our wedding, so he continued packing.

We danced around each other as we gathered his belongings. *Knock, knock.*

"Can you get the door, Sebastian? I think it's your parents."

Slowly moving toward the door, he hesitated to open it. He anticipated Scott might be with them. How right he was.

"Sebastian darling, offer help to your dad downstairs. He doesn't know where to park that piece of junk he just bought."

Charlene was not too impressed with her husband's choice of car.

"Sure, Mom, Nyria's in the room," he exchanged before heading down the stairs toward the back doors.

Charlene was excited to be a part of something that others could only dream about. Her son marrying an Earth girl who ended up being their Newbian queen.

"Nyria, honey, we're here."

Yelling from my bedroom, I hurried to greet her. "Sorry, I was just helping Sebastian pack his bag for the night. I don't think he wants to stay with Scott, even for an hour."

I was still giggling as I wrapped my left arm around my mother-in-law-to-be.

"I know how he feels. Scott was beginning to drive Bruce and me crazy."

There was absolutely no sarcasm in that statement.

"I know he can be a handful, but he means well. Scott has his own personality."

"That's for sure, dear."

Sebastian and Bruce were now standing at my apartment door with their hands full of decorations, luggage, and what looked like a cake-decorating book.

Bruce had a look of relief as he stood there waiting to be asked in.

"Go in, Dad." Sebastian said, bumping his father from behind.

Bruce made quite an entrance, unlike his wife.

"Hello, Nyria, you're looking beautiful as ever."

"Thank you, Bruce. Please put your things in the kitchen. We'll make room in my bedroom after you get settled."

The four of us began to talk about the big next day and how I wanted everything to go smoothly. Sebastian didn't talk too much, as he wanted me to have most of the say on how I wanted everything. This was my day!

He felt the happiness running through my body.

I remembered something. "Oh yeah, I forgot to tell you that the minister called. He asked if we could move the time to three p.m. tomorrow. He said something about a service being held at one p.m. I told him that would be fine. But we have to let the elders and Tyberrius know that the time has been changed. I think I told them two p.m."

Sebastian assured me he would notify everyone. That was the least he could do.

Before grabbing his bags, he placed his lips on mine, kissing passionately while telling me that Scott had something planned for him and to wish him luck.

Tucking his arms around my waist, he firmly pressed my body close to his. He glanced over my shoulder and told his parents he would see them later. He gave me one last kiss on my neck, then slowly moved toward the door before I wished him luck.

"Good luck. I don't want anything to be off tomorrow. Scott is one of a kind, Sebastian. Just take him with a grain of salt," I added, moving to the door and opening it while I perked my lips for a goodbye kiss again.

He placed his lips on mine while giving me a sloppy French kiss. We stayed locked together until his mother cleared her throat.

"See you all tomorrow."

"Bye!" I sighed while standing in the archway, watching him glance back with each step and blowing kisses at me. Closing the door behind me, I turned to find Charlene in the kitchen rummaging through my cupboards with a cake-decorating book open on the counter.

"I saw a cake in here that I think is absolutely gorgeous. Here Nyria, take a look."

I was curious to see what type of cake she picked out for us. It was beautiful. I wasn't sure if I wanted one made or store-bought. I gave a suggestion, but she interrupted me.

"No, no! Don't buy one. This is my gift to you. I want to make it. It's going to take me all day, but Sebastian told me you love the colour pink. So here I am. This jumped out at me. Do you like it, or do you want me to make—"

"No, no, this is perfect. I love it. Thank you!"

She smiled from ear to ear. I gazed at her as she searched for cookware, such a beautiful Newbian woman. I hoped to look like her when I reached her age.

"Do you need any help or anything?"

"No, Nyria. I brought some stuff from home. I wasn't sure if you had what I needed. You go relax."

I slowly moved out of the kitchen and joined Bruce sitting in the living room, looking through a Newbian magazine. He gestured for me to come sit with him. He wanted to show me something.

He was holding the magazine up for me to see a car decorated in pink ribbons.

"That's nice, but I was thinking maybe a horse and carriage. I love horses and, well, it's very romantic."

His eyes were wider than ever.

"That sounds excellent. Did you make reservations yet?"

"I did call one place and they are supposed to call me today."

"Well, if you'd like, I can ask Tyberrius to bring two of their horses with them. You won't have to worry about a no-show."

I couldn't believe they had horses, even though Newbia was another Earth-like planet. It seemed odd that my world was almost the same as theirs.

"They have horses? That would be great!"

I was delighted and felt more comfortable sitting beside him.

Hours went by as we made notes of what I wanted for the wedding. Charlene was busy making our wedding cake. We could hear her singing every once in a while as she banged and bumped around in the kitchen.

It was very calm and relaxing in the house with them. They were very sweet and kind. I could see where Sebastian got it from. His dad was quiet, but voiced his opinion, even though the final say was mine. Charlene would pop in smiling, covered in flour, then quickly dash back out to continue working on the cake.

The phone rang off the hook. Each time it was someone different. The first call was Lisa and Kevin, just reminding me they would be there and asking if I needed any help, but everything was under control, especially with his parents here.

I wondered what my two boys were up to, but didn't call to ask. Sebastian didn't call complaining about Scott. That was a good sign.

I could feel his emotions running wild with happiness. They were having a good time.

Once in a while, I knew Scott was up to no good. Sebastian would get angry, but it went away quickly.

Leave it to Scott, I thought to myself.

The night came fast. Charlene let out a loud sigh of relief, and called me in to see her masterpiece.

"Oh my. Wow, it's . . . um . . . beautiful, Charlene!"

Bruce stood behind me, nodding as if to say good job. I couldn't believe how beautiful and flawless it looked. Three layers of pound cake, with pink and white roses around the top and bottom. Three white pearls stemmed from each rose. Pillars held the layers high with light green vines wrapped around them with roses at each corner, always three roses in a bunch.

At the top of the cake there stood a slightly tan woman holding the hands of the man, almost as if they were dancing. Light green icing surrounded them like grass with roses at their feet.

"I thought I would give it a meadow look. Since you're getting married outside," Charlene said, waiting for my approval.

"I love it. It looks out of this world."

Everything about the Brinks and their kind was out of this world. They were very affectionate and loving in their own way.

"I'm glad you like it. Now you have to get some sleep, my dear. Tomorrow is coming quick," she mentioned while shoving me toward the bedroom.

"Yeah, I am a bit tired. I didn't make a bed for you two yet . . ."

"Don't worry about us, please. I'm sure Bruce will let me have a sofa." Bruce glanced over before adding that he would take the floor.

I asked if they wanted my bed and I would take the sofa. I was only one person and they could sleep together. But before I continued Charlene and Bruce both said no at the same time.

"We insist. You need your beauty sleep for tomorrow. By the way, do you have a wedding dress?" Charlene questioned.

"Yes, I have my mother's old wedding dress. It fits me perfectly. I guess we were the same size at twenty-four. Sebastian and I had a discussion about it. Oh yeah, and the rings . . . after my parents died, a lawyer came by with a will. In it, my mother and father asked if I would wear her dress and wedding ring. Sebastian will be wearing my father's. Do you want to see it?"

"We would love to." They smiling and joined their hands together, waiting patiently while I went to my bedroom. I retrieved it, opening the top dresser drawer and placing the diamond ring on my right index finger.

"Isn't it beautiful?"

Charlene and Bruce admired the ring before answering.

"Yes, it is gorgeous. Your mother and father will be happy!" Bruce managed to get out before heading to the kitchen.

"He always gets like this when it comes to marriages. His friend got married years ago and he was the same way. The man never cries, he just walks away before it happens. Don't take it personal."

I assured her I wouldn't. My father was the same way. I guess it was a manly thing.

Holding the rings close to my chest, I said my goodnights, gracefully closed my bedroom door and tucked myself into bed.

Together Forever

Rushing around was a little bit more difficult with three people in one small apartment. Still, we managed to get everything done before going to the Dartmouth Commons.

Karen and Lisa were waiting outside in their pastel-pink summer dresses, holding white roses.

Kevin was there in a beige tux with a pink dress shirt underneath.

They all stood still as I glided out of the building doors. Their mouths dropped to the ground. I was beautiful!

My hair was pinned up with white and pink roses around my bun. Strains of curls softly lay on my face. The wedding dress was all white with pearls swirling around it like ringlets. The train had a similar pattern. The pearls also went around the edges of it.

Karen started to cry as she saw my face light up with happiness.

"You look like a goddess! You're beautiful, Nyria."

Smiling, I thanked her and told everyone they were beautiful too. Kevin bowed his head and Lisa blew me a kiss. Charlene walked behind me, holding the train off the ground.

Bruce asked Kevin to help with the wedding cake, stacked in three large boxes.

We all climbed into our designated cars. I drove with Bruce and Charlene to the Dartmouth Commons. Tension and nervousness started to reign over me as I felt Sebastian's emotions climaxing. He was feeling the same way.

I tried to ignore it, but it became overpowering. Thinking of the baby and Newbia, everything was out of focus.

Arriving at the entrance, we saw everyone, including the minister, standing in a group. The minister was briefing them on what their roles would be.

Someone whispered, "She's here!"

They all took their places, sitting in white chairs with a pebbled path between the single rows that lead to the gazebo.

At the end of the path, Sebastian stood wearing an all-white Italian tux, fidgeting with his hands. He was nervous and eager to see me. His eyes began to water as he tried to reach over everyone on his tippy toes to see if he could catch a glimpse of me.

The wind was still as we marched down the pebbled path. Each took their seats as they approached the end.

The first to walk down was Karen. She threw white and pink petals along the ground and cried the whole way.

She smiled at Sebastian while moving her lips saying, "Take care of her for me."

Smiling back, he motioned the words, "Don't worry, I will."

Lisa and Kevin walked together hand in hand, with Sebastian's mother and father five steps behind them, shadowing my view.

As Lisa and Kevin broke from their march, Sebastian's parents stopped and smiled at their son, separating to give him a full view of me.

As I walked toward him holding a single white rose, a tear fell from my face. He almost lost his breath when his eyes focused on me. He has never seen beauty in this form before. He wanted to take me right then and there and run to the nearest bunch of trees to seduce me.

Feeling his emotions, I hesitated to move forward. Everyone froze as I stood still.

With Charlene close to me, I turned and whispered from the corner of my mouth, "If someone doesn't grab his attention right now, there will be no wedding. He's about to lunge at me and I can't seem to control him."

His mother's eyes grew bigger as I whispered my concern. She knew exactly what I meant. She too was once a seed and had to learn to block Sebastian's father from seducing her.

Turning quickly to her son, she snapped her fingers, breaking his spell.

"Stop it. Not here, not now."

Confusion washed over the faces of Karen and the minister, as they were the only ones who didn't know that they were surrounded by Newbians.

I quickly moved forward to take their attention off of their confusion. I reached Sebastian and he whispered, "You're the most beautiful woman in all the realms. I love you."

My eyes filled with tears while I whispered back, "I love you too."

Taking my hands in his, I felt the warmth of his heart shower me with love. I held him tighter than ever. His eyes were shining, holding back tears of happiness. I knew we were meant to be together.

"May we begin?" The minister asked.

Everyone fell quiet as he spoke.

"We gather here today to wed Ms. Nyria Crowell and Mr. Sebastian Brinks. If there is anyone who believes that they should not marry, speak now or forever hold their peace."

Sebastian and I did not move a muscle. We knew there was no one who could take this away from us.

The minister continued when no one said a word.

"Will you, Sebastian, have Nyria to be your wife? Will you love her, comfort and keep her and, forsaking all others, remain true to her as long as you both shall live?"

"I will."

"Will you, Nyria, have Sebastian to be your husband? Will you love him, comfort and keep him and, forsaking all others, remain true to him as long as you both shall live?"

"I will."

"The rings, please."

As he slipped the ring on my finger, my eyes told a story. He knew what they were saying. In return, I guided his ring onto his finger, and he licked his lips and uttered once again, "I love you."

"I now pronounce you husband and wife. You may kiss your bride."

With one hand embracing my face and the other wrapped around my back for support, he locked his lips onto mine. Everyone stood as they clapped and cried.

It was now time for us to climb aboard the horse and carriage that was waiting off in the distance to take us to our destination—a honeymoon in Jamaica.

Sebastian gracefully swooped me into his arms and ran to the carriage while I waved and blew kisses at everyone, especially Karen.

She would never see me again.

Reaching the horses, Sebastian asked me if I wanted to say goodbye to Karen one last time. Knowing it would be harder than just leaving without saying anything, I shook my head no. He kissed my cheek and laid me comfortably down on the seat, ordering the horses to ride.

"Wait, Sebastian. Tell the horses to go back. I want to give this rose to Karen. Even though she will never remember where it came from, I still want her to have it."

Without hesitating, he ordered the horses back. They trotted to Karen, coming to a full stop.

Leaning down, I handed the rose to Karen while saying, "Take care and thank you for everything. I will always love you."

Without giving Karen time to answer, we were off. Karen waved until we were out of sight.

Jules walked to Karen and asked her what she thought about the wedding, saying that she thought it was beautiful.

"Yes, it was. I'm so happy for Nyria. She's like a daughter to me."

Jules smiled, placed her hands on Karen's shoulders and uttered a spell to erase any memory of me.

"All that you've seen and known of Nyria Crowell is now gone."

The minister was next.

Reaching the end of the Dartmouth Commons, Sebastian ordered the horses to stop. Tyberrius was there to meet us.

Taking the horses by the lead, he wished us all the best.

Sebastian climbed down first, then turned to me with his arms open. I leaned forward and he grabbed me gently. He walked with me in his arms toward the gate.

He opened it to our honeymoon in Jamaica.

Last Day

As he threw the door open to our honeymoon suite, he gracefully placed me on the queen-size bed, whispering, "I can't hold it back much longer. You know when I get this feeling I can't control myself."

He crawled between my legs, opening them with the force of his biceps, and stared into my eyes.

"Let me play with your body. Enjoy what I'm about to do to you."

I felt his emotions rain all around me. It was hard to ignore. He kissed my thighs, taking my breath away. The tension of saying I do was now disappearing.

I loved to tease him, making it much more exciting. The submission will be well worth it, I thought to myself as I gave in to his demands.

I was lifted in the air, feeling the pleasure captivating my body. Gravity was trying to pull us back to the ground, but the pleasure behind his passion and the uncontrollable urge to make love to me was fighting with it to keep us levitated in the sexual feeling of paradise.

It lasted more than two hours until exhaustion set in. We lay there staring at the glass ceiling, taking deep breaths. Our eyes felt heavy as our breathing went back to normal.

Falling asleep in each other's arms, we dreamed of the perfect life together.

Waking up the next morning, we mauled each other getting into the shower. He caressed my belly, kissing me from head to toe.

Later, we decided to go whale watching. Other couples on the resort congratulated us on our marriage. We were surprised that so many people knew we were newlyweds. I guess the staff at the resort always made sure everyone knew who was who.

We were made aware of the other couples who were celebrating their weddings or anniversaries.

Whale watching was exciting. We saw a mother and calf swimming side by side while dolphins swam alongside the ship.

Holding me tight against his body, he could feel our baby kick me repeatedly. I didn't budge at the baby's kicks; they felt natural.

Sebastian would always search for the next kick. It was amazing how much the baby moved inside me.

During our honeymoon, there were times we seemed to be invisible, almost as if we were the only ones there, floating above the tallest trees, intertwined like the wind wrapping itself around the leaves, enjoying the views of Jamaica.

Neither of us had ever been there before. It was all new and exciting. Our love for one another grew with each passing minute.

Having dinner in restaurants that catered to us was very amusing. We laughed and giggled at each other as we whispered sweet nothings in each other's ears.

Colours danced around us, seen by only our eyes. It was beautiful.

Reaching our honeymoon suite once more, he stared into my eyes, demanding that I not block him. I didn't, for I wanted to enjoy all that he had to offer me. There was more to be felt when it came to lovemaking with him.

Knowing what I desired, he thrust himself deep inside me, making me scream his name over and over again as I bit his chest with every deep penetration. We felt the ground disappear below us as we levitated in the air. Colours rained over us as we made love, like always.

Feeling alive and radiant, he grabbed my hair and bit down on my neck, leaving faint teeth marks.

Admiring my expressions, he made love to me.

As we softly landed on the bed, I turned to him and gazed into his eyes, feeling that I was truly his seed—I was his soulmate and he was mine.

Our eyes fell closed at the same time as I laid across his chest. We fell deep into a restful sleep.

The next morning, I woke up to stomach pains.

I jumped out of bed, with Sebastian waking up from the pain himself.

I ran to the bathroom and began to vomit last night's supper.

"Nyria, sweetie, you OK?" he cried as he felt the pain within me. He grabbed my hair so I wouldn't get vomit in it.

"No, I—" I threw up again, loudly.

Feeling helpless, he stayed by my side and held my hair back, rubbing my back as I breathed between each session.

After five minutes of being sick, I glanced up at him standing over me.

"Sebastian, my water just broke!"

Shocked and surprised, he whisked me up into his arms and opened the realm to Newbia.

"We have to take you to the hospital to see Irene. Your water shouldn't have broken. You have another two months to go!"

Plunging through the realm, we found ourselves outside the hospital doors.

"Help, help!" Sebastian shouted until someone came to our aid.

Nurses and Irene came running.

"What wrong, Sebastian?"

"Her water broke!"

"What? Oh my, OK, bring her in." She pointed to a deserted room and Sebastian moved quickly.

Irene started ordering the nurses to grab warm blankets and equipment for the delivery. No sooner had she entered the room than I was yelling and twitching on the bed.

"The pain! The pain! I need something. *Now!*"

I took my PJs off. Irene said that she could see the head.

"I can't give you anything, Nyria. I can see the head. It won't do any good, he's coming. I need you to push when I say to, OK?"

Nodding in agreement, Irene told me to push.

Holding Sebastian's hand with one of mine and gripping his neck with the other, I gave it my all.

"OK, Nyria, you have to stop pushing," Irene ordered.

"I'm here Nyria, you can do this," Sebastian added while kissing my forehead, giving me his support.

Nurses were coming in and out, preparing for our baby's arrival.

"OK Nyria, *push!*"

I heard the baby cry.

Irene placed him on my chest while cutting and knotting the umbilical cord.

"Here he is, just gorgeous!"

My eyes filled with tears as I held my baby boy for the first time.

"He looks like you, Sebastian."

I cried as I stared at our new addition.

"Hi, little guy, I'm your daddy," he whispered, grabbing hold of his little fingers. Sebastian's eyes filled with joy at seeing our creation before him.

"What are you going to name him?"

Irene was now leaning toward my face, waiting for an answer.

Sebastian and I stared into each other's eyes, feeling each other's emotions. The connection was stronger than ever.

We hadn't discussed a name yet, but one fell off our lips as if we had.

"Constance."

Smiling in agreement, we repeated it again.

"Constance."

"Beautiful name. It's strong. I like it!" Irene was smiling from ear to ear. "I have to take him for a minute, though. I need to check his vitals and get him cleaned up. I will give him right back to you."

I handed him over and watched the little figure as Irene placed him on the tall clear holding table.

Sebastian kissed me over and over again, congratulating me on the delivery.

A nurse ran into the room.

"Something is going on outside. I think you should come with me, Sebastian."

All the faces in the room grew confused. We were all thinking the same thing: *What can be so pressing to interrupt such a beautiful moment?*

I thought something was wrong, but then again it could be his parents.

"Go see, Sebastian, it could be your parents. Plus, you can tell them we named him Constance," I suggested as I smiled at him, waiting for Irene to hand Constance back to me.

He gave me a kiss, then Constance, before exiting the room. He found himself walking toward the hospital doors with the nurse in full pursuit.

A crowd of Newbians shadowed his view as he approached. Pushing through to the front of the crowd, he saw what the commotion was all about.

Carmella!

"I told you I would be back when he was born. I want to see him," she uttered, stepping forward with a line of Lubrian warriors behind her.

Disgusted and angry, he voiced his disapproval.

"Never! Now leave, before I send my—"

Carmella cut him off before he could finish.

"Pfft! Do not flatter yourself, Sebastian. I'm not leaving without him."

No sooner did the words fall off her lips than a band of Newbian warriors surrounded them, Tyberrius taking centre stage.

Sebastian stepped toward Carmella with his hands folded across his chest.

"You're never getting your greasy little hands on my son. I think it's best for you and you're so-called warriors to leave."

Carmella stood firmly in her stance while mocking him. "I don't understand why you can't get it through your thick skull: I'm not leaving. So I guess you're going to have to tell them to attack."

Sebastian giggled at her bravery.

"There will be no fighting. We will win and you Lubrians will—"

Before he could finish, the sky grew dark, like a black sheet was covering it. Ships of Lubrians came in by the millions, filling the horizon.

Sebastian grew angrier with the sight.

"This is what you want? So be it!"

Raising his hands for all to see, he glared at his fellow Newbians and announced that war is at hand.

"Today we fight and today some die. We fight for . . ."

His warriors joined him:

"Newbia!"

CPSIA information can be obtained
at www.ICGtesting.com
Printed in the USA
LVHW090031091220
673679LV00006B/574